When Karim finally lifted his head they were both breathing hard. 'Oh, God!' Eva sighed, unpeeling her arms from his neck as he placed her back on her feet.

Karim gave a thin-lipped smile. 'You want it so badly you can taste it…' His voice trailed off as he looked at her and felt need flood through his body. He had never needed a woman…*wanted*, but not *needed*.

It was suddenly very important to Karim to prove this had not changed—that what he was feeling now was a reaction to the weeks of stress and the sudden release of tension.

'You want me so badly that you'll beg me to take you.'

The taunt brought a rosy flush of outrage to her cheeks. 'Never!' she choked.

Kim Lawrence lives on a farm in rural Anglesey. She runs two miles daily and finds this an excellent opportunity to unwind and seek inspiration for her writing! It also helps her keep up with her husband, two active sons, and the various stray animals which have adopted them. Always a fanatical consumer of fiction, she is now equally enthusiastic about writing. She loves a happy ending!

THE SHEIKH'S IMPATIENT VIRGIN

BY
KIM LAWRENCE

MILLS & BOON

First published in Great Britain 2009
Harlequin Mills & Boon Limited,
Eton House, 18-24 Paradise Road, Richmond, Surrey TW9 1SR

© Kim Lawrence 2009

ISBN: 978 0 263 87455 6

Set in Times Roman 10¼ on 11¼ pt
01-1209-53579

Printed and bound in Spain
by Litografia Rosés, S.A., Barcelona

THE SHEIKH'S
IMPATIENT
VIRGIN

To Peter, for telling me I can and learning to cook

CHAPTER ONE

'LET me get this straight.'

Luke was looking at her as though he expected her to produce a punchline.

'You're some sort of…' he paused for dramatic effect, pushing his floppy blond fringe from his eyes before adding with a half-smile '…princess? Princess Evie…?'

He chuckled.

Eva did not join him, but she had some sympathy for his skepticism. She had taken some convincing herself when on her mother's death the previous year a family she had not known existed had materialised—and not just any family!

She hooked her fingers into the belt loops of her jeans, stuck out her chin haughtily and tossed her plait over her shoulder before asking in a hurt voice, 'Are you saying I don't look regal?'

Luke Prentice could think of many terms, including *gorgeous* and *sexy* to describe the daughter of a woman who had been, in the small world of academia at least, a legend in her own lifetime.

He had no idea if Eva knew her mother had seduced him when he had been an eighteen-year-old student taking one of her classes to broaden his horizons—she had *definitely* broadened them—but he did know he stood no chance with the daughter, a situation Luke was philosophical about. Though he was something of a novice when it came to platonic relationships with women, he did find Eva's company kind of relaxing.

'I can't say I've ever associated freckles and red hair with Middle Eastern royalty before.'

Eva expelled a deep sigh and admitted, 'Me, neither.'

Even now it all seemed a little surreal. Her mother—her lovely, academically brilliant mother—had not been the single parent Eva had always believed, but the estranged wife of an Arab prince. Not a prince high in the pecking order, admittedly. The King, her grandfather—*King*, now *that* was still *seriously* weird—had produced nine sons and her father had been the youngest.

But he had been a prince and, as her uncle Hamid had explained when he had arrived at the funeral in his big black limousine with its bullet-proof windows, she was a princess, and he had produced the documentation to prove it.

Despite the fact her mother had always preached independence to her daughter, in a secret corner of her heart Eva had longed for a family, and now she had one. It had felt like fate when at the most terrible moment in her life and feeling utterly, totally alone she had found herself drawn into the heart of a large and exotic family.

Now of course she was learning there were drawbacks and a price for being part of this family. Still, she remained confident she could steer a course through this new obstacle diplomatically and maintain the relationship she valued with her grandfather.

'*Princess Eva…?* What is this really about, Evie?'

Eva struggled to contain her impatience. 'I've already told you.' Luke, the youngest professor of Economics in the history of the college, was not normally so slow on the uptake.

'But your mum wasn't married. Not that she was lacking male company…' He flashed Eva an apologetic look. 'No offence intended.'

'None taken,' Eva promised. Her mother had never attempted to hide her lovers, many considerably younger than herself. The relationships, or 'throwaway lovers' as her mother had termed them, had never lasted long, but unlike the rest, Luke had remained a friend.

It often struck Eva as ironic that her sexually liberated mother, who had discussed such matters with painful—for Eva at least—frankness, had produced a daughter who was still a virgin at twenty-three... Perhaps this was her own personal rebellion? On the other hand it was possible she just had a low sex drive—a depressing thought.

'It turns out she was, but she had a big bust-up with my dad.' A wistful expression drifted into Eva's eyes; she really wished she had had the opportunity to know him.

She had studied photos of him and the portrait that hung beside those of his brothers in the palace and could see no trace of him in her own features, but then there was little of her mother's classical beauty to be seen in her face, either.

Maybe she was a changeling? Though according to her mother Eva had inherited her fair skin, freckles and red hair from her own grandmother, who had been Irish.

'So they got divorced?'

Eva shook her head. 'No, he died in a boating accident before they could make the separation legal.'

Luke carried on looking astounded and not quite sure this was not part of some elaborate joke. 'And you didn't know any of this until your mum died?'

'No.'

'And now you want me to shack up with you?'

Eva frowned and snorted. 'In your dreams.'

This drew a grin from Luke, who shrugged and mused with a leer, 'How well you know me, Evie.'

'My grandfather thinks it's his duty to marry me off and before you say anything I know this is the twenty-first century, but that's the way he thinks. It's been instilled in him since birth that a woman needs the protection of her family or a husband.

I think in time he'll see that I'm more than capable of looking after myself, but I'm his only granddaughter. There's plenty of boys but I'm the only girl.' So Eva was making allowances and, to give him his due, so was her grandfather.

'In the meantime he'll force you to marry this guy who might have halitosis or a beer gut...'

'No beer,' Eva said, recalling that, beer or not, several of her male uncles and cousins carried more than a few extra pounds around their middles. 'Or for that matter, coercion.'

'But they do expect you to marry...what's his name?'

'Karim Al-Nasr,' Eva supplied, her brow puckering at the thought of her prospective spouse. He would certainly make a politically expedient husband.

King Hassan had obviously considered it a good sales pitch when he had brought babies into the conversation. Though Eva had no problem with babies—she definitely wanted some of her own one day—when they were mentioned in connection with a man she had never met, her first instinct was to run!

'No, they won't force me, but if I don't, which clearly I am not going to, it will feel like I'm throwing all their kindness and warmth back in their faces.

'I know it seems weird to you and me, Luke, but it is their way. I just thought it would be a lot easier if it was this Prince Karim who did the rejecting.'

'And you not being some innocent virgin is going to be a deal breaker, Eva?'

Her eyes dropped. 'They're very traditional.'

'Nobody's *that* traditional, Eva.'

Eva smiled and thought, *You'd be amazed*!

'This is, as you've already mentioned, the twenty-first century and you haven't spent the last twenty-three years in some cloistered desert palace.' His eyes made the journey from the top of her glossy head to her size-five feet and he sighed. 'Also you are exceptionally hot.'

Eva accepted the compliment and the mock leer that went

with it with a roll of her eyes and a dry, 'And they say romance is dead.' She didn't like the worryingly speculative light that had appeared in Luke's blue eyes as he removed his glasses and stared hard at her again. She could almost see the cogs turning as she added a shade uncomfortably, 'Shall we leave my sexual credentials out of this, Luke? Will you or won't you?'

'Pretend to be your live-in lover?' He carried on looking at her in a way that made Eva uneasy and loosed a laugh, adding, 'Try and stop me.'

Eva clapped her hands in relief. 'You're an angel.'

'And you're a virgin,' Luke announced, his grin broadening as her blush confirmed his suspicions. 'The girl who is writing her thesis on how the sexual revolution affects twenty-first-century woman is a virgin princess!' He rubbed his hands together gleefully. 'I just love it!'

'Shut up and put your razor in my bathroom.'

'Now that is an offer no man could refuse.'

The doctor, a physician renowned in the field of childhood cancers, did not normally feel apprehensive when he dealt sound advice to parents. Especially exhausted ones like this father, who had stood beside his daughter's bed for four days straight.

But he felt a tremor run through him as he approached the tall, imposing figure who, despite the fatigue that was etched in every line of his stern, hawkish features and the classic glassy look of total exhaustion in his disturbing penetrating platinum eyes, was standing ramrod straight, staring out of the window as the nurses made the slight figure in the bed comfortable.

Every so often he would turn and look at the figure, the pain in his eyes when he thought no one was observing belying the stern composure of his expression.

'Prince Karim?'

The tall man turned his head. 'There is news?'

The doctor, struggling to maintain eye contact, shook his head. This was not a man who looked as if he would be receptive to advice, and, though he gave the impression of someone who had iron control over his emotions, under the surface there was an almost *combustible* quality. This disturbing characteristic had become more conspicuous the longer he had gone without rest. 'As I said, Prince, we will not know the results until tomorrow.'

'But if the levels are within the safety parameters you will continue?'

The doctor nodded. 'We will, but you do realise that even if we are able to continue with the treatment, there are no guarantees... This treatment is still unproven.'

The man's cautious manner was beginning to irritate Karim. What was the point of caution at a time like this? A time when doing nothing would mean Amira died.

His thoughts veered sharply away from the possibility—the doctors warned probability—he utterly rejected. The muscle that ticked like a time bomb in his lean jaw was half hidden by the day's growth of stubble that shadowed his lower face as he clenched his fists at his sides and thought, *It will not happen.*

Ignoring the painful white light that exploded behind his eyes when he turned his head sharply and suppressing the primal urge to hit out, he responded with careful stilted courtesy to the medic.

'I am aware of the statistics, Doctor.' His glance slid to the heavily sedated figure in the bed, a person who had nothing to do with cold number-crunching, and he felt rage at the sheer helplessness of the situation. A man who normally had no problem facing the reality of a situation, he was breaking all his own rules.

It was his job to care for his child, to make her safe; relinquishing that role to others went against every instinct he had.

'Prince, I really think you should rest.'

'I'm fine.'

Despite his instant impatient dismissal of the suggestion, at one level Karim was aware that his vigil was beginning to have both physical and mental consequences.

His reflexes were slow, his thought processes...well, they were worse than slow. He struggled to concentrate on the simplest of tasks, and when he had signed the papers that Tariq had without explanation held out for his signature—Tariq had been a tower of silent, stolid strength—the tremor in his hand had rendered his signature virtually illegible.

'Your daughter does not know you are here. She is heavily sedated.'

Karim's lips compressed. He knew he would be of little use to his daughter if he could not function. 'I will be here when she wakes.'

'Of course, but in the meantime you could get a few hours' rest. We have rooms here...'

There was a pause before Karim reluctantly nodded his head.

The doctor, who had been standing there with his fingers crossed, let out a sigh of relief. 'Fine, I will arrange for—'

'Just give Tariq the details,' Karim said, already losing interest in the conversation as he walked back to his daughter's bedside.

The doctor, who found the man in question—an individual of indeterminate age who wore full traditional dress and possessed a face that looked as though it had been carved from granite—only slightly more approachable than his royal master, gave a weak smile of assent.

'The room is *adequate*,' Tariq said, managing despite his colourless tone to suggest that it was anything but. He inclined his head respectfully and held the door. 'I will wake you in four hours.'

'Two hours.'

'As you wish,' the man who was officially designated his

aide, but was in reality a great deal more, agreed, managing despite his respectful tone to convey extreme disapproval. 'I will position the guards at the end of the corridor. I have left a cup of tea by your bedside—it might help you sleep.'

'Fine,' Karim said, following the direction of Tariq's nod with his eyes but very little interest.

He was sure that had the guards decided to tap dance outside his room it wouldn't prevent him sleeping.

It turned out he was wrong. Far from sliding into blissful unconsciousness the moment he lay down, his brain went into overdrive.

For half an hour he lay there staring at the ceiling, tasting the bitter aftertaste left by the herbal tea he had obediently swallowed even though he hated the stuff, a fact Tariq was aware of—it was an uncharacteristic oversight on his part. He was conscious of an intense overwhelming weariness in every cell of his body, but his brain just wouldn't turn off.

Karim's thoughts continued to go around in nightmarish circles until finally he snapped his fingers and inhaled. 'Enough is enough!' he said as he levered himself into an upright position, ignoring as he did so the extra throb of pain in his head.

He glanced at the metal-banded watch on his wrist as he shrugged on the jacket he had dropped on a chair, then, dragging a hand through his hair, walked to the door.

He might, he decided, take a walk outside before he returned to Amira's room.

As he emerged into the corridor the guards stationed down at the far end remained unconscious of his approach; halfway there he stopped and retraced his steps. If he was going to take a walk to clear his head and escape the claustrophobic hospital atmosphere, it would be pleasant for once in his life not to have his steps dogged.

Amazingly Karim encountered no one else as he made his way to the conveniently placed fire exit, down the steps and out of the building. It was raining outside but he barely registered the moisture streaming down his face as he began to walk across the gravel, his thoughts drifting back over the weeks since Amira had been diagnosed.

It barely seemed credible that only a month ago his life had been normal, a mere four weeks since he had first noticed the purple shadows beneath her eyes…*how long had they been there?*

What sort of father did not *know* such a thing?

Pushing aside the guilt he inevitably felt when he considered the shortcomings in his parenting skills, he recalled bringing up the subject with Amira's governess.

'It seems to me that Amira has been tired often lately?' He waited, wanting her to politely dismiss his comment as that of an overanxious parent.

She didn't.

The suggestion initially brought a slight defensive stiffening to the middle-aged woman's narrow shoulders, then as she considered his words Karim saw a speaking flicker of concern cross her face.

His own unease immediately solidified into apprehension.

'Well, I suppose she has seemed a little lethargic lately…' she conceded. 'But she's an active child….'

Not active enough to explain the bruises he had seen on her arms.

Karim felt an icy fist of dread clutch in his belly. It was not his custom to waste time worrying about problems that might not even exist, but where his daughter was concerned his normal practice went out of the window.

When Amira had been born, Karim had been determined that the child should not suffer for her mother's deception or his own stupidity. He would, he had decided, act towards the child that bore his name the same way he would have had she been his flesh and blood—which as far as the rest of the world was concerned she was.

When the baby had arrived eight months after the wedding

most had pretended not to be able to do the maths, though his father had given his son an indulgent wry look and commented on the impatience of the young, and his cousins had indulged in the odd joking comment. Their reactions might have been less amused if they had known the truth—if they had known that, far from anticipating his wedding vows, he had never slept with his wife, who had chosen their wedding night to inform him that she was carrying another man's child.

Despite this vow Karim had never expected to *feel* the emotions that a man felt for his own child, but he had been wrong. Her mother had lain still heavily sedated when the screaming wet bundle had been placed in his arms and he had been utterly unprepared for the rush of feeling that had washed over him.

The screaming red-faced scrap had seemed to look directly at him, and by the time she had stopped crying Karim's heart had been firmly in the clenched little baby fist.

The baby was now eight and the situation had not changed, except since her mother's death two years earlier he was the only one who knew the secret—Amira was not his biological daughter.

Now the doctor knew. When the subject of marrow donation had arisen Karim had been forced to admit that it was unlikely he would be suitable, and then responding to the medic's tactful probing he had revealed that he had no idea who her biological father was.

For the first time he had cause to bitterly regret his lack of interest in the identity of his wife's married lover. If he had asked the question there might be someone out there who could help Amira.

But he hadn't asked.

Of course, if he had loved Zara, Karim might have wanted to torture himself with the details, but he had not. And a day did not go by that Karim was not grateful for this and his apparent inability to fall in love. History was littered by men left destroyed and humbled when the women they loved had cheated and deceived them.

It was not a situation that Karim ever intended to place himself in. If he ever had been a romantic his marriage had opened his eyes to the dangers of that condition. No, he would marry for duty; for love or, rather, sex, he would look elsewhere.

CHAPTER TWO

WHEN he spotted the car parked on the kerb on the other side of the narrow road, Karim's first thought was that his bodyguard escort had seen him leaving the precinct of the hospital earlier... How much earlier?

He frowned as he attempted to clear the fog in his brain and tried to think... Why could he not think? His glance drifted downwards, and the permanent groove between his darkly delineated eyebrows deepened. He was wet. He brushed a hand across the fabric of his saturated suit and said out loud, 'Very wet.'

Suggesting...suggesting what? Karim, struggling to make the mental connection, lifted his face to the rain. He stood there with it streaming over his face and realised he had no conscious recollection of leaving the hospital precinct. He felt a surge of impatience. Presumably, as he had not just materialised here, he had done so. What was that taste in his mouth?

Of course...Tariq's tea—he had slipped away to get some air.

To get some air, but he had obviously got more air than he'd intended and, though he had unintentionally escaped the hospital precinct, he had not escaped the dark thoughts that gnawed with the merciless precision of a surgical blade into his head— he had brought them with him.

He had to get back from here, but where, he wondered,

scanning the street he found himself in, was here? He recognised nothing, including the men in the parked car. Men who would, if they were any good at their job, have noticed him before he had registered them.

They were paid to be observant; they were paid when required to blend into the background. They were blending and if he had not been watched and guarded all his life, Karim would not have given the anonymous vehicle a second glance—but he had.

It said a lot about his frame of mind that he only glanced with mild curiosity towards the building they were watching as he squinted in the dim light to bring the name on the red brick façade into focus.

Church Mansions…a grand name for a not very grand building, a typical Edwardian villa divided like most in the street into flats. The groove between his dark brows deepened as he impatiently pushed away a hank of wet hair that dripped a steady stream of water droplets into his eyes from his forehead.

Now why, he puzzled, did that name seem familiar? And why could he not string two syllables together, let alone two thoughts?

Then as he was turning to retrace his steps it hit him: this was where King Hassan's granddaughter lived. This was the address where on Thursday evening he had been meant to pick her up. The arrangement had been made prior to Amira's diagnosis—presumably Tariq, his right-hand man, had made his apologies.

What day was it now? Thursday, no Friday…just, and now he was here, led by what…fate?

Karim did not believe in the arbitrary hand of providence; the idea of not being in charge of his own destiny was total anathema to him. A man made his own fate; he took responsibility for his own decisions, the bad ones and the good ones.

Was this a bad one? he wondered as he scanned the names on the doorplate until he found the one he was searching for.

There was a logical reason for his decision, though in truth at that moment it eluded him, but it would be logical and probably to do with duty. He shook his head in the vain hope of clearing his tangled thoughts—the lift wasn't working so he took the stairs—his life involved a lot of duty.

It had been duty that had made him agree to the meeting with this girl, the meeting that had never happened.

He had agreed out of duty and respect for Hassan Al-Hakim, King of Azharim, a country that shared a border with Zuhaymi. The two desert states had been allies for many years, as had the royal families, but before that they had been traditional enemies.

King Hassan was not the first to suggest that it was time he married again, but he was the first to actually suggest a possible bride.

'You don't need me to point out your duty, Karim, but while you are without a wife every politically ambitious ruling family lives in hope, they plot and connive. Being born who you are has given you status, power and wealth, but at a price. A hereditary leader's first duty is to his country and people. They look to you for stability, a sense of continuity and permanence—an heir…'

'And preferably a couple of spares.'

His flippancy, though not appreciated, had been tolerated, but it was not in the same league as refusing to meet the granddaughter of his neighbour with a view to marriage. Such an insult might not have returned the respective countries to war status, but it would have strained the relationship, so Karim had been willing to go through the motions and treat the suggestion with the gravity it did not deserve.

Karim could readily appreciate the King's desire to see his granddaughter married, and of course by birth this girl fulfilled all the criteria for a royal bride.

But birth was not the only consideration.

Karim was one of the few who were privy to the story of the

lost princess who had been ignorant of her birthright. It made for good romance and an even better headline when the media found out, which to his mind was inevitable. But to expect a woman brought up knowing nothing of tradition to take on such a role as his wife would be called upon to perform would be like expecting a ten-year-old to conduct a lecture on astrophysics!

Karim knew he had to marry and his expectations were realistic. He was not expecting to find a soul mate to make his wife—if such things existed outside the pages of romances—though someone who didn't actively dislike the idea of sharing his bed would be a step up from the first time.

But the lost princess would not be his first or last choice.

And anyway there was no hurry—he was enjoying his freedom and he was only thirty-two. Young, but not as young as some—Amira was eight.

And he would have given all he had to exchange places with her. An image of her little face beneath the cap she'd taken to wearing since the chemo had made her sweet curls fall out flashed across his vision. If ever he had been under the illusion that life was either fair or certain he had learnt otherwise over the past weeks.

Pushing aside the dark thoughts, he concentrated on taking the next shallow, slightly shabby step and then the next. Best not to think too far ahead…marriage too was far in the future. Why marry now when he was enjoying his freedom, and enjoying sex without guilt or responsibility? He mentally skimmed over the post-coital emptiness that, had he been a man given to introspection, might have bothered him.

Of course, if Amira had been a boy things would have been different. Marriage would not be on his agenda and there would not be the ever-present pressure from those advising him to marry.

Karim did not need others to point out his duty. He would eventually have to remarry and provide the much-desired heir.

His face relaxed into a half-smile that briefly warmed the bleakness of his platinum eyes as his thoughts returned to his daughter. It amazed him that two people who could only make each other so unhappy had produced such a marvellous, perfect little creature.

It was 1:00 a.m. when Eva decided to head for a shower as she was too wound up and plain mad to sleep. Irrational really. It wasn't as if she'd wanted him to turn up, but bad manners were bad manners even if she had no complaint about the result.

Her night had started badly and gone steadily downhill. For starters her computer had crashed and she'd lost a week's work, and then the manager in the hotel bar where she worked to supplement her adequate but not generous post-grad funding had rung to ask her to cover a shift.

An offer she'd had to refuse so next time he wouldn't ask her first, and with her computer on the blink she could do with the cash. Not that she was really broke—the startlingly generous allowance her grandfather had insisted on making her was sitting in the bank where it was going to stay. Using it somehow felt too much like relinquishing her freedom.

God, this entire day had been a waste. As if she didn't have anything better to do than spend hours deciding what to wear that was completely unsuitable and more hours artistically arranging Luke's personal items in her bathroom and several articles of his clothing around her flat to suggest cohabitation.

Of course she should have recognised the Prince wasn't exactly keen as mustard when a flunky had rung to arrange the date a month previously—he clearly had a busy calendar.

'Damn man!' she muttered, kicking off her shoes. In a mood of righteous indignation she removed the rest of her unsuitable outfit. 'Who does the man think he is anyway? Other than rich and powerful…obviously common courtesy and good manners don't apply to royalty.'

It was just a pity, she reflected, that not all the men in her life were letting her down tonight.

Luke had arrived on cue. 'Where is he?'

'Not here.'

Her tetchy tone had not been lost on Luke, who had not done the tactful thing and vanished but instead had hung around, wanting the gruesome details, enjoying immensely the joke at her expense.

Eva liked to think that she didn't take herself seriously, that she could laugh at herself with the best, but there were limits and someone laughing his socks off because she'd been stood up was definitely over her limit.

She'd been pretty cranky and terribly unappreciative with Luke, but anyone who observed with a grin, 'Looks like the guy is not as enthusiastic as you thought, Princess,' in her opinion deserved cranky!

Luke had carried on digging the hole when he'd added, 'You've got to appreciate the irony, Evie!'

At this point Eva had opened the door and invited him to leave, ignoring the jibe about a sense-of-humour bypass.

As she stepped into the shower, Eva decided to draw a line under the entire 'prince's prospective bride' scenario. If the wretched man's flunky rang back to schedule a meeting again, she would be washing her hair.

In the meantime she was revolving in the warm spray of the shower when she heard the strident shrill of the doorbell.

Damn! It would be Luke, who, since he had made the big move out to the leafy suburbs, had got into the annoying habit of using her sofa when he had missed his last train home. Well, actually, she didn't normally find it annoying, but tonight she wasn't feeling exactly hospitable.

Lifting her face briefly to the water to rinse off the remnants of soap, she pulled off the shower cap and shook out her hair before fighting her way into a towelling robe, muttering, 'Hold your horses,' under her breath as she dashed to answer the door.

This time her sofa was *not* going to be available even if Luke did the 'pathetic puppy dog' look.

Her problem, she told herself, was she was too damned *nice*, and niceness, as her mother had always told her, was an open invitation for people to walk all over you.

Was it any wonder she got stood up? She clearly sent out victim messages even over the phone!

Mid-mental rant, she came to an abrupt halt when she saw the shadow of a large figure through the frosted glass of the door.

Too large to be Luke?

Surely the damned Prince wouldn't have the cheek to think she'd still be dutifully waiting until he deigned to show up? Her eyes narrowed wrathfully at the idea as she reached up and slid the bolt on the door. In his world did women wait patiently? Eva's temper fizzed. For sheer, mind-numbing vanity, this man really did take the cake.

Sucking in a deep sustaining breath, she really couldn't wait to explain that she only gave a man one chance and he'd blown his. Pleased with the line, she closed her eyes before pinning a combative smile on her face and checking the towelling robe was covering everything it ought. It was and more—it reached her toes.

She opened the door with a flourish.

The tall figure who had been standing with his back to the door turned and Eva's vocal cords froze. Actually pretty much everything she had, including her ability to think—correction, *especially* her ability to think—froze.

CHAPTER THREE

FOR some reason Eva had been expecting the Prince to in some way resemble the royal male relatives of her new family—well, he was both male and royal—who were squarely built men whose height enabled them to carry the extra pounds that most did indeed carry.

The man she tilted her head up to look at was indeed tall but he had no spare pounds. Not that Eva immediately registered his lean, athletic frame—it was his face that initially totally transfixed her.

Never had she expected to connect beauty to a face that was so essentially masculine—if you made an exception for the sweep of those curling ebony eyelashes that any woman would have traded an inch of cleavage for.

But he was beautiful, each sybaritic carved line and sculpted angle of the face she gazed at, from the sternly sensual mouth, slashing cheekbones, strong jaw, strongly defined dark brows to the spookily silver—*really silver*—eyes was without flaw. Even his skin was flawless, a deep even gold.

Eva gathered her wits and, expelling a tiny gusty sigh, closed her mouth with an audible click. Her lashes came down in a protective screen as she dropped her chin and took a deep sustaining breath.

This was really her prince?

The one her grandfather had conceded was *quite* good-looking when pressed.

Well, not *hers*, obviously. Men like this did not *belong* to women who looked like her, though *belonged* was actually the wrong word. *Belonged* implied a degree of domestication that she was unable to mentally connect with this feral, though admittedly completely magnificent creature.

He might be dressed in western clothes, but this was not his natural habitat. It was not a leap to imagine him framed against a cerulean desert sky, his tall, lean frame covered in flowing desert robes.

Eva imagined it and felt her stomach muscles quiver at the sybaritic image…what was her grandfather thinking of? Suitable match, he'd said! *Suitable*? For heaven's sake, they were about as suited as an Arab stallion and a shaggy Shetland pony!

One thing was clear, she realised as she lifted her chin and tried to collect her wits, her elaborate plans to convince him she was unsuitable were fairly pointless. This tall man who oozed male arrogance from every perfect pore was not going to buy what was on offer.

On offer…like I'm a commodity on a market stall! Eva's temper cut through the thrall that had held her immobile. She opened her mouth to say something cold and cutting, but before she could the eyes that had been focused on some place over her left shoulder suddenly connected with her own.

The unfocused blankness and lack of recognition, the pain mirrored in those silvery depths, sent the words from her head.

The last time she had seen an expression like that it had been in the eyes of a young man who had stood watching the car he had been thrown from consumed by tongues of orange flames.

'I should be in that,' he had said over and over when Eva, along with another driver who had pulled off the road to help, had tried to pull him back from the heat.

Shock, the paramedics, after one glance at the shivering figure, had explained as they led him to the ambulance.

She angled an assessing glance at her late-night caller, and struggled to be objective. It was hard when the person you were trying to be objective about oozed animal magnetism.... It was frankly distracting even for someone like her, who did not go for the muscular macho type.

As she continued to subject the strong lines of his handsome face to a critical scrutiny the last sparks of annoyance in her green eyes morphed into anxiety. Despite that sinfully sexy mouth he did have the look of the walking wounded.

Had the Prince done the equivalent of walking away from a burning car? She was no paramedic, but the man standing there looking back at her but, she suspected, not actually seeing her seemed to be suffering from a similar trauma. And if the purple shadows under his eyes and the deep lines of strain bracketing his sensual mouth were any indicator, galloping exhaustion.

Concern conquered caution, common sense and instinct—the latter was telling her to close the door. She heaved a sigh and tried to inject a note of enthusiasm into her voice as she said abruptly, 'You'd better come inside. I'm assuming you are the Prince?' It didn't seem a big assumption considering the hauteur he projected even in this clearly tormented condition.

He started slightly at the sound of her voice as if he'd forgotten she was there and his glazed eyes narrowed on her face. Eva was conscious of a strange sensation trickling down her spine.

'I'm Karim Al-Nasr.' The furrow between his dark brows deepened as his eyes swept her upturned features. There was too much intelligence lurking in those troubled depths to call his expression vacant, but he continued to look at her with an uncomprehending lack of recognition and the sensation she had noted stopped being a tickle and turned into a flood that spread out across her skin, crackling like an unearthed electrical current just beneath the surface.

'I'm not sure why I'm here.' His eyes narrowed to silver slits. 'Do I know you?' His voice dropped to little more than a husky murmur as his veiled glance brushed across her bright head, following the fall of the tousled curls as they fell down her shoulders. It made the fine hair on Eva's arms stand on end.

'Red hair, like flames…'

Heavens! The man could invite sin with a single syllable.

Eve had read of bedroom voices, but this was the first time she'd ever heard one—deep with an abrasive rasp beneath the rich velvet smoothness that was wickedly seductive.

'I wouldn't have forgotten that.'

He sounded as positive as she had yet heard him about this and Eva self-consciously reached a hand to drag a tangled Titian skein from her face.

'Once seen never forgotten.' Which for some people might be a good thing, but for someone like Eva, who didn't enjoy drawing attention to herself, it was not. 'We had a date, Prince,' she reminded him bluntly.

And after all the names she had called him it looked as if he had a legitimate excuse not to show. What she wasn't sure of was why he had shown up now, here of all places.

The frown that dug grooves into his broad smooth forehead tugged his strongly defined ebony brows into a straight line above his patrician nose.

'Did we…? Yes, you're King Hassan's lost princess…' The comprehension that had flared in his eyes faded as he appeared to lose track of what he was saying once more.

From the look on his face Eva got the strong impression that the place his thoughts had gone was not fun. *Lost*, he'd called her—it looked to Eva as if he were the lost one!

As she watched he swayed slightly and put out a hand to steady himself, clearly dead on his feet. Struggling against a swell of empathy, Eva let the hand she'd instinctively raised fall back to her side.

Even though her next move was obvious and Eva had never had trouble extending a helping hand to someone in trouble in her life, continuing to encourage this man over her threshold was one of the hardest things she had ever done.

Not only was she utterly sure that under normal circumstances he was the total antithesis of vulnerable, but she knew—every instinct, particularly the ones that did not work on a logical level, was telling her—that the kindly gesture would have unforeseen repercussions.

You're being dramatic, Eva, she told herself, squaring her shoulders and murmuring, 'Get a grip.' Anyway, what choice did she have? She could hardly close the door in his face. Gritting her teeth, she took a sustaining gulp of air and, reaching out, laid a hand tentatively on his arm.

He appeared not to notice the hand, but she noticed the muscular hardness—it was hard to miss.

'Come inside, erm…Prince,' she said, pitching her voice to a soothing level as her fingers closed over muscles that did not give. *Bad idea,* said the voice in her head as her unselective stomach muscles responded to the innocent contact with a less than innocent series of butterfly kicks.

'Inside…?' she repeated hoarsely.

After a moment he responded. Eva's relief was short-lived as the voice in her head very legitimately asked once more, *What do you think you're doing, Eva?*

She said, 'Duck,' a moment too late and he didn't. The top of his dark head—the man towered over her; he had to be at least six four—connected in a glancing blow that he appeared not to notice with the doorjamb.

'Oh, my God, be careful!' she groaned.

Explaining a royal prince with a fractured skull to the emergency services would really make the day complete.

'Are you all right?'

'All right?' Karim repeated, lifting a hand to his head. His fingers came away damp and stained red. He couldn't feel a thing, he felt weirdly disconnected from his body. Sleep deprivation, he thought as he made a concerted effort to clear the

fog in his brain and in a moment of lucidity thought this was more than lack of sleep. Before he could figure what the more was, the moment passed.

He still retained the recognition that he ought not to be here. He was meant to be at the hospital… Amira was there and his inability to do anything was driving him slowly out of his mind.

How ironic was it he could influence the political stability of an entire region with a few well-considered words, he could transform the day to save the lives of an entire community by delivering power and running water, but when it came to his own child he was powerless…he had to stand and watch as she endured pain…as *she slipped away from him*?

He should prepare himself. Karim closed his eyes, rejecting the advice.

Preparing implied a resignation that he did not and would not feel.

'I should go,' he said, inhaling the scent of this woman's body and wanting not to stop.

Please, Eva thought, and immediately felt guilty. It was odd, but when she looked at him her usually abundant kindness to strangers went out of the window. Any number of other things happened when she looked, but Eva was grimly determined not to go there.

Where's your heart, Eva? she asked herself. She wouldn't show a stray cat the door looking as he did. Of course, he wasn't a stray cat, and if he had been this would have been a lot simpler.

'I think you should sit down for a moment, Mr…Prince.' The title sounded so ludicrous she fought off a smile. Then as she tilted her head back to look into his face, she lost all desire to smile… He really was stupendous to look at. 'I could call a doctor…?'

'No doctor!' The hazy look was gone from the eyes that drilled into her like silvered surgical scalpels.

'All right,' she said, not willing to push the point. It was, after all, none of her business. 'A cup of tea, then.'

'A cup of tea?' he repeated with a frown.

'I don't have anything stronger,' she said apologetically, thinking, More's the pity. She could do with something to steady her nerves.

His glazed gaze strayed from her face, wandered towards her hair, and an expression of edgy fascination that made her heart rate quicken spread across his lean face.

He lifted his hand and reached out. The gesture had all the hallmarks of compulsion as he touched her hair. Eva stiffened and thought, *Don't just stand there, do something*, as she felt the light pressure of his long fingers moving across the silky surface.

In her head she had pulled back; in reality she stayed nailed to the spot, her heart racing as he lifted one strand and then another and let them fall through his fingers. As his brown fingers sank deeper, grazing her scalp, a tremor that reached her toes passed through Eva's body.

'Like silk...a flame...'

His voice broke the spell and with a gasp she stepped back, breathing hard. She dragged both hands through her hair, tucking it behind her ears as she tightened the knot on her towel and cleared her throat. The entire 'naked under the layer of towelling' thing had intensified the illicit thrill of being touched with such casual intimacy by this incredible-looking stranger.

'Look, I think...' She stopped. He wasn't looking, at least not at her, which was a relief. It made it easier for her to think, not to mention breathe. If what this man exuded like a force field could be isolated and marketed no woman would be safe!

And she'd invited him in. *Really great idea, Eva*!

'Sit down,' she suggested hopefully—if he didn't move of his own accord, she was in trouble. He was a big man and all of it was solid muscle.

Do not go there, Eva, she told herself as her stomach flipped.

'For God's sake, sit down or…' She felt alarm and then relief when he took a step away from the sofa and folded his long length into her overstuffed wing-backed armchair. 'Great.'

Now what, Eva?

Eva turned a deaf ear to the unhelpful voice and, frowning and praying for inspiration, dropped down on her knees beside the chair.

'Are you all right?' Eva rolled her eyes and bit her lip thinking, *Sure, he's great, Eva—that's why he's sitting there with his face in his hands.*

She ground her teeth in sheer frustration. This man probably had an entire army of people to look after him. Why had she decided to play Florence Nightingale? She wasn't even very good at it!

'Is there someone I can call for you?' She laid a tentative hand on his arm and felt the vibration of the invisible tremors that ran through his tense body. 'My God, you're wet through!' she exclaimed, belatedly registering his wet hair and even wetter clothes. 'We should get you out of these things, erm, sheikh…Prince.' She stopped the mental image in her head causing colour to flood her face. 'Maybe not…' she added hoarsely as she sat back on her heels.

She swallowed as her eyes were drawn of their own volition to the golden skin of his throat where his tie had been pulled askew. His saturated white shirt clung like a second skin and Eva, seeing the shadow through it of dark body hair on his chest, averted her eyes quickly, but not before her stomach had lurched.

She scrambled hastily to her feet—at least he was in no condition to notice the scalding blush of shame that washed over her skin.

'You wait there. I'll get you something dry.' Her eyes flickered to the blood on his forehead. 'And something to put on that head.' She cast a worried look at the blood oozing from the small but seemingly deep cut on his forehead. 'Don't move,' she added sternly as she tightened the towelling robe across her heaving bosom and ran from the room, not waiting to see if her words had registered with him.

She really needed some time out to regain her equilibrium. In the bedroom she closed the door and leaned against it with her eyes closed. She lifted a hand to her head. It was shaking and her palm was clammy with nervous sweat. Maybe it was a proximity thing but she had never encountered anyone that had such a *visceral* effect on her before.

Not the best time for her dormant hormones to kick in. She had to...what...? She frowned in concentration and struggled to focus her thoughts. For a start get some clothes on. She pulled on the fresh pair of pyjamas laid out on the bed.

What she needed, she decided, picking up a tartan throw from the bed, was a number of someone to call for him. Or even an address and she could call a taxi and put him in it. Calling her grandfather's number for advice was the very last resort. She was still shaky on royal protocol, but she was assuming it was a given that her present situation broke several rules and, though they had cut her a lot of slack and put down several of her worst faux pas to ignorance, this might be pushing it.

She ducked into her tiny en-suite shower room and snatched up a couple of towels from the linen hamper before heading back into the sitting room.

CHAPTER FOUR

'I've got…' She stopped, her mouth falling open as the towel fell from her nerveless fingers.

On autopilot, she stepped over the wet shirt and jacket on the floor and whispered hoarsely, *'Oh, God!'*

Her agitated comment went unheard because her guest, his dark head cushioned against the wing-back armchair, was asleep.

Deeply asleep.

Deeply asleep and half naked, the upper half.

Thank God for small mercies!

A laugh that had more than a hint of hysteria in it left her throat as Eva ran her tongue across her dry lips. There was a naked man in her sitting room—a naked man who had a body that would have put the average Greek god to shame.

Feeling like a voyeur but unable to stop herself, Eva gazed curiously over the sleeping figure. He lay half on his side, one arm flung above his head. His build was powerful but greyhound lean, and he didn't carry an ounce of excess flesh on his gleaming torso to conceal the perfect muscular development of his broad chest, powerful shoulders and muscle-ridged flat belly.

He had the perfectly toned body of an athlete at the height of his powers.

Eva approached, breath held. Up closer she could see that

the even bronze of his skin had a satiny gleam. It reminded her of dull gold. The light dusting of body hair on his chest terminated in a thin line that ran across his belly and, like a directional arrow, then vanished into the waistband of his trousers. His powerful chest rose and fell in time with the sound of his deep, regular breathing.

Her own breathing was less even as she willed her eyes not to follow that arrow. It was extremely fortunate—considering the effect his naked torso had on her nervous system—that he appeared to have fallen asleep *before* he got any farther than his shirt.

Eva started guiltily as he moaned in his sleep and shifted his position, causing a lot of muscle rippling that sent a lustful stab of longing through Eva's helplessly responsive body.

Her face burning with guilt, she carefully draped the throw over him, avoiding all form of skin-to-skin contact as she pulled it up to cover his shoulders and, her eyes still on him, bent to pick up the wet clothes scattered around the room.

She did not need the hand-stitched labels to tell her they had not come off any peg. In the act of raising the silk fabric of his shirt to her face to inhale the subtle fragrance that she had noticed, she froze when she realised what she was doing.

'You have a problem, girl!' she told herself as she folded his clothes neatly at arm's length and placed them over the back of a chair. She cast a last look at the sleeping figure before switching off the lights and tiptoeing, though heaven knew he seemed dead to the world, towards the door. Hand on the handle, she turned back, and by the light shining under the door from her bedroom retraced her steps and flicked on the lamp beside the sleeping figure.

This time her glance lingered. She couldn't help herself. His face in repose exerted an almost hypnotic fascination for her from the chiselled angle of his high cheekbones to the contrasting soft sweep of his lashes. And his mouth… Swallowing, she

dragged her gaze clear of the sensually sculpted outline and expelled a shaky sigh. He really was an astonishing-looking man.

Eva had never understood the attraction herself, but they did
say that power and wealth, both of which he apparently had in
abundance, were aphrodisiacs—but frankly he didn't need any
assistance. If Prince Karim Al-Nasr had been born just plain
Joe Bloggs and his worldly possessions only consisted of that
mouth he'd collect women as a honeypot collected bees!

Eva found herself wondering about women. Was there a
particular one who woke up looking at that face, maybe seeing
that mouth smile? Those eyes smoulder with need? Would his
marriage alter that situation?

The unsettled line of speculation sent a rush of heat through
Eva's body, but despite the hot prickle under her skin she was
shivering as, feeling ridiculously like a thief in the night, which
was pretty crazy considering this was her flat and he was the
intruder, she crept back to her bedroom.

This time she didn't look back.

She wasn't exactly amazed when sleep eluded her. Her over-
active brain kept replaying the strange events that had led to a
man being asleep in the next room.

A man her grandfather would have liked to see her married
to. Up until this point she had considered King Hassan a fairly
rational man. She shook her head. The evening had not been
what she had anticipated, but who could have foreseen what had
actually happened?

As she lay tossing and getting hot, sticky and tangled in her
pyjamas, Eva was plagued by doubts that she had done the right
thing.

What if he was concussed or worse?

She could have invited a homicidal maniac into her home.

She comforted herself with the fact if he was he was in no
condition to do her much harm and, to her admittedly untrained
eye, his condition appeared to have more to do with sleep deprivation than anything more life threatening. His colour had

seemed healthy as he lay sleeping and he had been quite clear on the subject of medical assistance.

She wondered a little about his seeming aversion to doctors.

She shook her head impatiently. If she was going to lie in her bed, reading something into every syllable he had uttered and every expression, she was never going to sleep. The answer was probably as simple as the man had just been partying too hard.

Not that he had looked the self-indulgent type, unless that indulgence was sex, she thought, her stomach muscles quivering as an image of his face floated before her eyes. The aura of raw sensuality and power he projected did not suggest he was exactly a stranger to carnal pleasures. It was an aura that Eva was glad she had not walked into unprepared when he wasn't in a physically weakened condition.

In the morning, after sleep, he would probably be back to his normal self, whatever his normal self was. Eva couldn't help but be mildly curious.

She toyed with the idea of going back into the room to check on his condition, but after a sly voice in her head cast some doubt on her motivation, she decided against this action.

At some point Eva did fall into a fitful sleep. When she woke it was morning and the light was filtering through her curtains. She gave a sleepy yawn, began to stretch, then suddenly the events of the early hours came flooding back and she was fully awake.

At almost the same moment the memories surfaced she became aware of the mattress creaking gently, only she wasn't moving. She carried on *not* moving as her heart rate picked up and she recognised the sound of someone breathing and it wasn't her!

The sound was very close. It was… She swallowed convulsively and fought down an inappropriate desire to laugh—a normal person would have screamed. There was someone in her room. The mattress gave way…there was someone in her bed!

Hysteria a heartbeat away and not daring to move or open her eyes, Eva tried to breathe quietly as horror steadily ate into her fragile control.

Well, you can't just lie here, woman—do something! Heart thudding, she forced herself to open her eyes.

Oh, my God!

Even though she had been half prepared it was still a shock to her nervous system to see Prince Karim Al-Nasr, his dark head lying on the pillow beside her.

His breathing suggested he wasn't going to wake up any time soon—her first break. All she had to do was get out of bed without him noticing—the simplest plans were always the best—and a lot of embarrassment would be spared all round.

Her racing thoughts, not racing as fast as her heart, reconstructed a probable scenario that had ended with him in her bed. Stumbling around his unfamiliar surroundings half asleep in the night the Prince had presumably stumbled his way into her bed…or rather any bed—it just happened to be hers.

Nothing personal, it wasn't the lure of my body. A bubble of hysteria rose in her throat as she pressed a hand to her lips. She finally had a man in her bed. Of course, he was unconscious and she hadn't intended for him to be there, so possibly it didn't count.

Eva, her wide eyes fixed on the sleeping man, began to surreptitiously ease herself away from the sleeping prince and towards the edge of the bed.

She was tantalisingly close to achieving her goal when the sleeping figure moaned in his sleep and shifted his position.

Dismayed, she looked down at the arm that he had thrown across her waist. A second later a heavily muscled thigh followed and she was effectively pinned to the bed.

She was reviewing her options when he reached out blindly and pulled her to him. Their bodies collided, her softer one automatically moulding itself with startling ease to his hard contours.

Shock held her momentarily immobile, then something else stopped her from pulling back.

The something had a lot to do with the intoxicating novelty of being held this intimately close to a hard male—or was it just this male in particular?

The disturbing question was for another time when her mind was not being bombarded with so many new and exciting sensations. Her nostrils flared as her senses responded, independent of her brain, hungrily to the musky male scent of his warm body.

Eva had never thought about how different the male body was from her own. She lay there now, her breath coming in short, shallow, painful gasps, thinking about it, thinking about how seductive the differences were—hard instead of soft and the solid weight of a male body. She wondered about being under that weight, feeling it press her into the mattress, and felt her temperature spike—or was that him? Eva felt sure that if she touched his skin it would burn her…not that she would, of course, because that would be wrong on too many levels to count, and, besides, not a good idea. She needed to cool down, not inflame an already dangerously inflammatory situation.

What I need is distance and plenty of it.

Eva swallowed and tried unsuccessfully to ease her leg from under his; she needed to be somewhere safe from the musky male scent of his body.

The thought was there but not the will to carry it through. Drowning in the sensual lethargy that made her feel intensely aware yet simultaneously strangely disconnected from her own body and what was happening to it, she got fatally distracted by the length of his eyelashes.

Training her gaze on this relatively safe area of his anatomy, she examined with growing fascination his eyelashes. Dark against the angle of his high cheekbones, a hank of dark glossy hair had fallen across his face.

Eva had actually lifted her hand with the intention of pushing it back—this felt as if it were happening to someone else…but it wasn't!

What was she doing?

Face burning with shame, she began to pull away. As she did so his grip tightened. She felt rather than heard the groan that vibrated in his chest and panicked… He was waking up!

Clumsy in her haste, her elbow connected with his ribs. She was muttering a mortified, 'Sorry,' while trying to slide out from under the weight of his arm when, without warning, he buried his face in her neck.

Thoughts of escape went out of the window along with common sense. Her tightly closed eyelids fluttered as she felt his mouth on her neck. Then his hand was pushing under her shirt and closing over her breast and everything inside her melted as his thumb moved across her sensitised nipple and a feral moan was dragged from somewhere deep inside her.

'No…yes…this is…' Eva made a token attempt to move, but only managed to get her fingers tangled in his hair.

She wanted to make love to a total stranger—*wanted* barely began to cover the driving urgency that blitzed along her nerve endings through her veins. The realisation shocked her back to reality.

What are you doing, Eva? Whatever it was it was incredible. 'Wake up!'

She was afraid her plea did not carry the conviction it ought, but it seemed to have some effect. He stopped nuzzling her neck and lifted his head.

Eva could never be sure in what order the next three events occurred, but his slumberous eyes opened and connected with hers.

She heard herself say stupidly, 'I'm Eva. How's your head, Mr…Prince?'

And Luke walked in, his eyes trained on the two takeaway coffees and a carton of croissants he was balancing.

'I knocked, no answer. I let myself in—a peace offering. Do you know you're late for your tutorial, Evie?'

Luke's head lifted and his eyes opened wider than seemed physically possible as he saw the couple in the bed. His eyebrows shot to his hairline as he murmured, 'Oops!' And did a three-hundred-and-sixty-degree turn before exiting.

Eva gave an anguished groan as she sat up in bed, scarlet to the roots of her hair, and yelled after him, 'This isn't what it looks like, Luke!'

'He is particularly gullible, then, your boyfriend? Or just the forgiving kind?'

Eva looked down at the man lying in the bed beside her, one arm curved over his head, the other touching the gash on his head. Gone was the air of vulnerability and vagueness of the previous evening; replacing it was a sardonic expression and a remarkably expressive and deeply unpleasant sneer.

He didn't look forgiving; he looked like a man who held grudges.

There was a time lapse of several seconds before she realised that his eyes were trained on her gaping top.

Hating the blush that rose to the roots of her hair, Eva bunched the fabric of her top in one hand and, flinging off the duvet with the other, leapt out of bed. Her expression of indignant reproach produced a bold grin that revealed even white teeth and contained no hint of repentance for the ogling—not that she had a lot to ogle.

Not that she gave a damn how this stranger rated her breasts, because that would make her needy and mildly pathetic.

'Last night…' she began, struggling to look like someone who took waking up with a man in her bed in her stride, '…you were…'

'Last night…' he echoed.

Eva saw the sudden recognition flash into his eyes and watched as the sardonic amusement faded abruptly.

'You're Hassan's lost princess.'

'I'm not lost. I live here.'

He flashed a less than enthusiastic look around the room and said, 'But you're planning on moving up in the world, aren't you, Princess?'

The rather cryptic observation brought a distracted frown to Eva's brow…distracted because she was conscious of the background clatter as Luke slipped the latch on her front door.

'I won't be a minute.' She gave an apologetic grimace and snatched up her robe from a chair.

'I do not have a minute,' Karim observed grimly.

His guilt climbed as he thought of his extended absence…his recollection was hazy, but one fact was inescapable: he had presumably, in some aberrant moment of unforgivable, shameful weakness, walked, or at least wandered, away from his responsibilities.

If he was not there when Amira woke he would never forgive himself.

The glance he slid her had the chill factor of an arctic front and Eva couldn't help but contrast his present manner with the heat of his lips on her neck and the urgency in his hard, hot body as it had pressed into hers minutes earlier.

'What time is it?' he snapped, throwing aside the covers and vaulting with fluid grace from the bed.

Eva tried not to stare. His body stood up well to daylight scrutiny. Perfect was like that, she thought with a sigh. His eagerness to be gone was not exactly flattering to her ego, but his departure could not, she told herself, be too soon for her.

'I don't know.'

The honest response drew a forbidding frown.

'Look, I won't be a second…' she called back as she ran to catch Luke. While she was answerable to nobody about whom she shared her bed with—up to this point no one—she felt an urgent need to put the record straight, and she really didn't want Luke to leave with the wrong idea.

CHAPTER FIVE

KARIM walked into the minuscule sitting room, his eyes moving immediately to the face of the clock sitting on the mantle. He grimaced and felt a fresh surge of guilt when he thought of Amira waking up and him not being there.

And why wouldn't he be there? Even with hazy recall the answer did not require hours of deep analysis—it was right there in the waking impressions that lingered in his head.

Lithe pale limbs, warm soft curves, skin like satin and a supple body curved into his.

His mouth curved into a grimace of self-contempt even as his body hardened in response to the memory. During the barren years of marriage he had turned control of his passions into an art form, but inexplicably that control had deserted him at the worst possible moment.

A muscle worked in his lean jaw emphasising the hollows beneath his strongly etched cheekbones as Karim considered what the moment of inexplicable weakness combined with the scheming of a woman was going to cost him.

The irony was he couldn't even remember the pleasure he was about to pay so dearly for—that part of the night remained a total blank.

The same could not be said for all of the night. A brooding frown on his face, he walked to the window and glanced down at the street below. Any faint hopes he nurtured that this specific section of intact memory was not real died an instant death.

The stationary car opposite was depressingly real. He turned away and wondered how long it would take for the information his granddaughter had spent the night with Karim Al-Nasr to reach King Hassan.

Of the King's reaction there was no similar question. While the ruler of Azharim was not a man who was averse to change, tradition and honour were two things he placed highly. Karim had offered him an insult and only one response would make that insult forgivable.

Karim closed his eyes and, his expression harsh with self-recrimination, wondered if there was a fatal flaw in his make-up.

Was he preordained to make the same mistake over and over again? Recognising the self-pity insidiously creeping into his thinking, he pushed away the thought, firm in his belief such a mindset was for men who could not accept responsibility for their own actions.

No excuses, no extenuating circumstances and no amount of extraordinary red hair changed the fact he had messed up and he would pay.

The depth of his own stupidity was still hard for him to fully grasp. He inhaled through flared nostrils and, exerting the control that had let him down the previous night, he pushed away a subject he had no time to explore right now and estimated how long it would take him to get to the hospital.

He found his jacket and retrieved the phone from the pocket, punched in a number while shrugging on his shirt. The dampness brought back the memory of rain…and walking.

Tariq picked up immediately.

Karim, his shoulder hunched to hold the phone while he buttoned his shirt, was thrown by the deep sigh of relief that reverberated down the line. His calm and ultra-composed right hand then threw him some more when Tariq proceeded to launch into a breathless emotional monologue that inexplicably involved a central theme of choked, almost *tearful* self-recrimination.

When he began to repeat himself Karim, bemused by the uncharacteristic overreaction, felt it time to interrupt.

'I'm sorry I gave Security the slip, but you are hardly responsible for that, and I am no longer a child, Tariq.' Tariq, who had known him since he was assigned bodyguard duty when Karim was ten, sometimes had to be gently reminded of this. 'I can look after myself.' Though after last night this was open to debate.

Far from being soothed, Tariq appeared even more agitated when he replied, 'When the room was discovered empty we did not know where you had gone and I thought… This is my fault. I am so sorry. I did what I thought was best.'

Karim's bemused frown deepened. *'Best?'*

'You recall that sedation…the sleeping draft the hospital doctor prescribed…'

'I recall throwing it away.' Karim was not a fan of quick fixes and even less of numbed emotions. He would face what he must with all his wits about him and sleep, when it came, would be natural, not drug-induced.

'I retrieved it.'

'You retrieved it,' Karim echoed, his tone neutral as the last piece of the puzzle he hadn't known existed clicked into place in his head.

It was a very loud click! And things made more sense. Not that being drugged counted as a 'get out of jail' card when applied to sleeping with a royal princess of a close political ally.

'Yes, and I put it in the tea.'

Karim exhaled. The tea…at least now he knew why he had been wandering the streets. It had not been temporary insanity brought on by stress; it had been drugs!

'I was most afraid that you had come to some harm….'

You have no idea, old friend, Karim thought, pressing the

phone to his chest. He knew it would be a mistake to speak at that moment and say something he might regret…even though it would make him feel a lot better in the short term!

The idea that anyone thought they knew what was best for him did not sit well at any time with Karim, but the knowledge that this particular piece of monumental interference was going to have dire consequences only increased his level of outrage.

If it had been *anyone* else but Tariq who had been watching his back since he was a child, anyone else but Tariq who clearly already was consumed with guilt…

He closed his eyes and, lifting the phone, reminded himself that it was weakness to yell at someone who was not in a position to yell back.

'That was very resourceful of you.'

'Of course I will formally submit my resignation and in the meantime—'

Karim, his tone brisk and impatient, cut across the stilted speech. 'In the *meantime*, Tariq, you will send a car to flat 11 A Church Mansions, and if you drug me again we will definitely fall out….'

There was a pause before he heard a fervent, 'Yes, Prince Karim.'

How could he punish a man who always had his best interest at heart, a man who offered him unswerving loyalty? 'Is Amira awake yet…?'

'No…no…she is still asleep. Church Mansions…is that not the address of King Hassan's gran—?'

'Yes, it is. You, Tariq, can be the first to congratulate me, and if King Hassan tries to contact me before I return send him my compliments and tell him I will speak to him personally at the first opportunity.'

He was sliding his phone back into his pocket when the sound of voices in the hallway that had been a constant background noise stopped. Into the ensuing silence he heard a distinctive click as the door closed.

Karim sensed rather than heard her enter the room. He could feel her eyes on him but did not immediately turn his head. When he did she froze in the act of taking a step towards him, uncertainty reflected in her emerald-green eyes. For a moment her eyes held his, then her eyes and her half-outstretched hand fell in unison.

Karim turned his gaze from her burnished head, conscious as he did so of the rage and hunger so deeply entwined when he looked at her that attempting to separate the emotions was pointless.

'Luke's gone.' And to her annoyance he hadn't believed a word she'd said.

Oh, well, there was a silver lining at least. Now Luke was not going to be spreading stories about her alleged virginity— any sniggers were going to be about one-night stands, which was, as it happened, marginally less embarrassing.

Karim's cold expression hid the anger he struggled to contain as he retrieved his jacket from the back of a chair.

'I have somewhere I need to be. I'm late. We will discuss this situation later.'

The man could multitask, Eva thought, clasping her hands protectively across her chest. He could shrug on his jacket and simultaneously send her a look that most people reserved for something nasty on their shoe.

She was bemused by his attitude and found being viewed with such acute distaste not pleasant, though for all she knew, this might be his normal expression. While she hadn't expected thanks for not throwing him out the previous evening, a little civility would not, in her opinion, have been out of place.

'There's nothing much to discuss, is there?'

In the act of fastening the middle button on his jacket he paused and, one brow raised, shot her a look that brimmed with icy incredulity.

Puzzled by his inexplicable hostility, she shrugged and said,

'Well, there isn't.' For all she knew this might be the norm for him, which had to make him a positive delight to be around.

'Drop the innocent act.'

The terse advice made her blink owlishly up at him. As she did she was conscious where his gaze was levelled. The slow burning blush began like a prickle under her skin and worked its way out until her body was suffused by a rosy glow as she pulled her flapping robe across her chest and belted it firmly.

The top button of her pyjama top was presumably in the bed somewhere. Trying very hard not to think about how it had ended up there, she lifted her chin and retorted, 'Look, I'd love to trade insults, but I don't know what you mean.'

'I have no taste for play-acting.' His frown still in place, he reached inside his jacket with a frown.

When he withdrew his hand a pair of boxer shorts that had been spoiling the line of his perfect tailoring appeared.

Crawling out of her skin with embarrassment, Eva wondered if she wished hard enough would she vanish…?

He held the bright red boxers with the strategically placed suggestive logo out as though they carried a contagious disease, the film of icy contempt in his stunning eyes deepening as he observed, 'Not mine, I think.'

Definitely not his, but the problem was Eva could see him in them and actually, as her imagination took another unscheduled leap, without them.

I am losing my mind—it is the only explanation.

Struggling to adopt an expression that did not scream 'I'm thinking about you naked,' Eva looked at Luke's borrowed item of clothing swinging from his fingers and felt the blush extend to every part of her anatomy.

Was it really only yesterday that arranging Luke's personal items around the flat had seemed like a brilliant idea?

She had opened her mouth to offer a hurried explanation when she thought, *Why should I? What right does he have to look down on me from that great moral height?*

She was willing to bet that when it came to moral depravity he could teach her a thing or two. Her gaze drifted to his mouth, drawn by the overtly sensual sculpted curve of his lips, and she thought, Probably considerably more than two!

She blinked to clear the sensual fog that was thickening in her brain and wondered if there was some physiological reason for this explosion of ill-timed hormonal activity as she lifted her chin and schooled her expression into neutrality, murmuring a soft thank-you.

He looked visibly taken aback by the quiet dignity of her response, but the flicker of uncertainty didn't last. Eva wasn't surprised—he was obviously not the type of man to doubt his own judgement and his judgement of her was clearly that she was some sort of predatory trollop!

In any other circumstances this fatally flawed casting might have appealed to Eva's lively sense of humour, but nothing about this acutely uncomfortable situation made her feel like smiling.

While Karim had been enjoying his freedom with a series of like-minded ladies, he had never suffered a moment's unease thinking about their previous lovers. So he was totally unprepared for the lick of sheer rage produced by the mental image of the faceless men who had occupied Eva's bed before him. Unable to banish the image of another man's hands caressing her taut, high breasts, Karim struggled for control as his emotions flamed higher.

'You must have quite a healthy lost-property box.'

Her startled glance flew to his face and, registering the condemnation there, she embraced the rush of anger filling her as she snatched the boxers from his fingers.

Keeping her combative glare trained on his face, she squeezed them up into a ball and pushed them into her dressing-gown pocket.

'I'm not the lost one.'

He didn't look lost now, either—he looked like someone she

would not have invited into her home. A secret shiver slid down her spine… He had danger written all over him.

'And if it's reputation you're worrying about,' she suggested calmly, 'don't. Luke won't say anything.'

She hoped resolving to stress her request that he keep this to himself at the first opportunity. Luke had many fine qualities, but she knew that the ability to keep a good story to himself was not one of them.

'So *Luke* is the owner of…?' Karim gave a sharp nod towards the red fabric sticking out of her pocket.

Watching his nostrils quiver with distaste, Eva folded her arms across her chest, wondering who made him the Chief Justice of good taste?

If he wanted to think she had so many men she couldn't keep track of their underclothes, let him, she thought as she admitted, 'Well, I wouldn't *swear* to it, but they are his sort of thing. Luke,' she added, defiance slipping into her voice, 'is a friend.'

Hate was a strong word for a strong emotion, but this man wasn't a person who inspired tepid. Her expression set stiffly, she walked to the sitting-room door and held it open in invitation, saying with a smile that left her eyes unfriendly, 'I'd say it has been a pleasure but…' She deepened the smile, raised her brows and let her scorn show as she gave a suggestive shrug.

'I fail to understand your unfriendly mood. You have achieved what you set out to…'

Her feathery brows knitted as she angled a questioning look at him. 'What have I achieved?'

'You might find marriage is not what you expect.'

'Marriage?' she parroted, oozing a hoarse laugh. 'Are you mad? Or is that your idea of a joke? There is not going to be any marriage. I only agreed to see you because my grandfather asked me to. I was just being polite.'

Karim nodded towards the open bedroom door and allowed his grin to widen. 'You have an interesting take on polite.'

Eva stared at him in horror. 'You think we slept together?'

Her dismay appeared so genuine that Karim was forced to consider for the first time the unlikely possibility that she had genuinely not thought of the consequences when she had allowed him to share her bed.

Such a hedonistic attitude to life was alien to Karim, who could not remember a time when he had not known his actions had consequences. If this lost princess really thought she could carry on as she had she was facing a rude awakening and very steep learning curve!

He for one thought the rude awakening was overdue.

'It is an assumption I make when I wake up in a woman's bed.'

Eva's eyes narrowed. Nasty sarcastic rat! 'You really do think you're a catch, don't you? Well, for your information, this time you'd be wrong with your assumption,' Eva told him, skimming over the uncomfortable fact that if Luke had arrived any later her footing on the moral high ground might be less secure.

'I was not capable?' He looked amused rather than chastened by the idea.

'I really wouldn't know what you were capable of!' she retorted, acutely uncomfortable by the direction this conversation was taking. From his tone he might have been discussing the price of milk, not his sexual performance, which was a subject she wanted to leave well alone. 'And I had no desire to find out,' she assured him with a disdainful sniff.

He struggled to contain his impatience at this blatant falsehood. Presumably she thought she could gain something, what he had no idea, by acting as if the sexual tension between them that even now was an almost tangible presence in the room did not exist.

'So *that* is the message you were trying to send when you were groping me.' He gave a cynical smile as his glance drifted over her slim body; he was enjoying empty sex outside marriage and it appeared he could carry on enjoying the same thing inside marriage. 'I can see now it was just a matter of crossed wires.'

His sardonic sneer drew a mortified squeak from Eva. '*You* were groping *me*.' She swallowed and lowered her eyes as the memory of his lips on her skin, his hand on... *Do not go there, Eva*! 'I woke up and found you in my bed. I suppose you'd sleepwalked or something, and then you grabbed me.'

He heard her out with an infuriating air of polite scepticism and then suggested, 'And you fought off my advances?'

Eva compressed her lips, looked at him with seething dislike, but did not make the mistake of tackling that issue. Instead she just repeated the bare facts.

'We did not sleep together, end of story. You were...' An image of his appearance the previous night flashed into her head and she admitted, 'Well, actually, I don't know what you *were*, you looked terrible, and before I could find out what was wrong you fell asleep in that chair.'

She walked to the armchair, where it seemed she could see the outline of his body in the cushions, and punched the armrest wishing it were him.

'You tell a nice story and I would like to suspend disbelief— but...' He gave a fluid shrug.

Eva rolled her eyes heavenward. '*But* you don't believe a word I'm saying.'

He shrugged again and touched a booted foot to the shabby chair as, eyes sparkling with platinum scorn, he held her eyes. 'That's not where I woke up, *ma belle*.'

'And I don't sleep with men I've just met, especially when they are egotistical, arrogant—'

'*Liking* is not necessary for good sex. I thought we were a good...fit.'

The husky interruption sent a surge of heat through Eva's body. The effort of *not* looking at him brought a fine film of sweat to her brow, but she was only delaying the inevitable. The compulsion to look at him proved too strong to resist and their eyes clashed, emerald on metallic silver.

She felt as if a fist had reached into her chest and while she wondered if this was what dying felt like she watched his eyes darken, the pupils widening until only silver rims remained.

Eva didn't know how long she stood paralysed by lust until the hand she gripped the chair with slipped and sent a cushion tumbling to the floor, where it knocked over a half burnt candle in the hearth occupied by an ugly old electric fire.

'All right, I'll come clean—I took advantage of you in your weakened condition,' Eva drawled, taking refuge in sarcasm.

'That's a lot more likely than me sleepwalking my way into your bed.'

'You can't actually think I want to marry you?' The man had to be deluded, incredibly sexy but deluded. 'Look, as I've already said, I only agreed to meet you to be polite, because my grandfather...' She broke off and gave a choked laugh. 'God knows how he thought we'd suit...but I imagine he sees an entirely different side of you.'

His eyes narrowed to silver slits. 'I imagine that he sees an entirely different side of you too. I have no idea why he tolerates your lifestyle. I certainly will not.'

This casually autocratic warning drew a squeak of outrage from an incredulous Eva.

'Look, you saw an opportunity and you took it.' Karim passed a hand across his face. Eva, who didn't want to feel any empathy for this man, ignored the weariness of the gesture. 'I cannot blame you for that.'

Eva blinked at the concession and opened her mouth to ask him what on earth he was talking about when he added, 'But do not expect me to admire you, Princess. We had our fun and now we both have to pay the price—'

'I had no fun!'

Her shrill interruption drew a look of irritation from him.

'You know as well as I do that when your grandfather learns we spent the night together…'

Lifting her hands to her head in an attitude of utter frustration, Eva was driven to stamping her foot as she ground from between clenched teeth, 'I keep telling you nothing happened. Absolutely nothing! Why doesn't anyone believe me?'

'What I believe is not relevant. King Hassan—'

'King Hassan won't know unless you tell him.'

Karim's jaw clenched as her pointless display of fake naïveté pushed his patience to the limit and a little way beyond.

'That really won't be necessary. I imagine your bodyguards will already have made a full report.'

Eva's chin went up and, though she continued to glare, there was a sparkle of triumph in her eyes as she replied evenly, 'I don't have bodyguards. I'm kind of new to the princess stuff but my grandfather knows I'm more than capable of looking after myself.'

'So the men sitting in the car across the street are decorative?'

Eva looked at him blankly. 'Car?' She struggled not to laugh. 'What car?'

He nodded towards the window. 'That car.'

'It's a street. People park.' Just to humour him she walked towards the window and glanced out; the nondescript black hatchback parked on the kerb opposite was the first thing she saw.

In the act of swinging back to him she paused, a frown of disquiet forming on her smooth brow as she searched her memory. Hadn't the same car been there last night…or yesterday or both…?

'Surely you have noticed that car or one similar before.'

Eva tilted her face to his, ignoring the twinge of uncertainty, and she gave a scornful laugh, which unfortunately emerged as a panicky squeak.

'Why would I need a team of bodyguards?' The idea that

people had been watching her every move sent a shudder of distaste down her spine.

'Because you are the granddaughter of a king, because there are security issues, because…' He arched a brow. 'Shall I go on?'

'Nobody knows who I am…' Eva struggled to hide the flutter of panic his suggestions had caused, then, regaining perspective, added, 'I'm not really a princess. It was just an accident of birth.'

'I can't decide,' he mused, studying her face, 'if you're in denial or just stupid.'

'And I can't decide if you work at being a total pain in the neck or it comes naturally.'

The seamless rebuttal stopped Karim in his tracks. So, apparently people didn't tell him he was a pain on a regular basis. Pity—a bit of humility might make him almost human.

Struggling to slow her laboured breathing, she raised her hands and waved her slender bare fingers at him.

'Look, no jewels, no crown,' she added, and pressed her hands to her burnished gold head. 'I'm not really royal.' She shook her bright head from side to side, adding, 'I never even knew my dad.'

'He was by all accounts a good man.'

Momentarily distracted by the comment, Eva lifted her eyes eagerly to his face. *'Really?'*

The wistfulness in her voice—she clearly had no idea it was there—hit Karim in a vulnerable corner of his heart. Refusing to recognise the feeling that swept through him as empathy, he nodded abruptly.

'But you never met him?'

'When I was a child,' he admitted.

Eva's chest lifted in a soft sigh that was audible. Karim searched her face, a part of him perversely *wanting* to see some sign that she was dissembling, that the emotion and the vulnerability were false, but he found none.

Up until this point he had viewed her unconventional up-bringing as a soft option. She had spent her life free of the re-strictions and responsibilities that came with being born into a royal family, the restrictions he had lived with all his life. Now for the first time he recognised the possibility that she had missed out too.

'I wish I had met him…I—' She caught him staring at her and, feeling suddenly self-conscious and exposed—his eyes did have that 'strip a soul bare' quality—she lifted her chin and gave a soft gurgle of laughter.

'It's not as if anyone is going to write about me in the tab-loids or kidnap me!'

She nearly had him until the seductively suggestive laugh that made the hairs on his neck stand on end in primal aware-ness. Nobody who laughed that way could be that naïve!

'So you had no idea you've had a team of men following you for weeks.'

'Months,' she corrected, going pale as her stomach churned in sick rejection of the possibility. 'I've been back home for two months.' The first week or so she had been a bit nervous that the news would leak and she'd be the victim of intrusive in-terest, but when nothing had happened or changed she had relaxed.

Until now!

Her resentful glance lifted to the dark sardonic face of her overnight guest.

'Are you calling me a liar? Are you…?' She stopped, the col-our seeping from her face leaving spots of angry pink on her smooth cheeks.

Her green eyes flashed as she said in a deceptively quiet voice, 'You think I knew that they were there reporting, you think I let you stay here because I wanted to compromise you…'

'So such a thing did not cross your mind.'

'You think I planned…how?' she demanded, waving a furious finger of triumph at him as she saw the flaw in his accusation. 'Even if I wanted to marry you, and let me tell you I'd prefer to remove my spleen with a spoon, how was I to know you'd turn up on my doorstep in the middle of the night, looking like a…?' She paused, losing some of her focus as she recalled the haunted bleakness in his eyes.

He gave an impatient shrug and picked a bleeping mobile phone from his pocket. 'I am not accusing you of being a mastermind, just an opportunist.' His eyes scanned the phone. 'This will have to wait. I'm late.'

Annoyed at the implication that anything he was late for would automatically be more important than anything she had planned brought a glitter of dislike to Eva's green eyes—the man had an ego the size of a continent!

And if he looked down his nose at her again, prince or no prince, she was going to sock that supercilious, superior smirk off his face.

The good thing about being mad with him was she didn't have to think about her shameful physical response to him—and being mad with him didn't even require any effort on her part.

'Well, I'm so sorry your schedule is thrown,' she sympathised with saccharin-sweet insincerity, 'but I didn't invite you to stay the night.

'Though of course you wouldn't remember that,' she added sarcastically.

It seemed to Eva his selective recall was awfully convenient and she was starting to tire of being made to feel like some sort of scarlet woman.

'And if I don't get a move on I'll be late for work too.'

'Work…?'

He said it as though it was an alien concept. Maybe it was to him?

Maybe he had someone to tie his shoelaces? Maybe he strode around all day looking enigmatic and masterful?

'Yes.'

'I thought you were a student.'

'I am, but like most students, even ones with scholarships,' she added, trying to hide her pride in the achievement, 'I have a job. Two actually. I work in a bar and walk dogs.'

His dark brows twitched into a straight line above his hawkish nose. 'I'm amazed your grandfather permits it.'

'I didn't ask his permission.'

'And surely you do not *need* to work.'

Her expression hardened at the suggestion she was a sponger. 'I can pay my own way…and I value my independence. I'm not looking for *anyone*,' she said, emphasising the word, 'to look after me.'

'And I, *ma belle*, also value my independence, and I was not looking for a wife, but sometimes a man must make the best of an imperfect situation.'

Eva gave a gasp of wrathful indignation. 'Some people would not think marrying me such an awful thing.'

Standing in the doorway, he turned back.

Eva shivered as his heavy-lidded eyes moved slowly across the soft angles of her heart-shaped face. 'I can see,' he admitted, 'how that might happen.' With a last enigmatic non-smiling look, he turned and left without a word.

She expelled the breath she had been holding in one gusty sigh. You had to hand it to the man—he knew how to do an exit! And that cryptic parting comment, what was that about…? Was *he* saying he would like to marry her?

Not that she cared. Right?

A frown knitting her brow, Eva walked slowly to the window. As she looked down onto the street below she saw Karim emerge.

As she tried to analyse what it was about the way he moved that made something as simple as walking across the street riveting she saw him approach the stationary vehicle.

He tapped the roof and almost immediately two beefy figures emerged.

She gave a little grunt of satisfaction at the sight of the men dressed in jeans and tee shirts. There was nothing at all covert about them; he was wrong!

Her feeling of smug triumph lasted as long as it took them to start bowing obsequiously towards Karim. Even when they stopped their body language remained visibly respectful.

They spoke, or rather listened, for several minutes, then got back into the car.

Karim turned his head and glanced up to her building. Eva guiltily jumped back, biting her lip and almost groaning when she thought about what a fool she must have looked, and she waited a few minutes before looking back out.

There was no sign of Karim or the men in the car.

'Well...' she sighed heavily '...I think you could safely say that that date did not go well.'

CHAPTER SIX

Lost in her thoughts, her hood pulled over her head to protect against the rain, Eva didn't see the long, low car with the blacked-out windows until it slowed down, spraying her skirt and boots with muddy water.

'Great!' She still had one more dog to deliver to its owner and didn't know if she would have time to go back to the flat to change before she started her shift in the hotel bar.

'Get in!'

The terse order made her stumble and forget her wet skirt and mud-spattered legs and the tiny dog she had popped into the conveniently big pocket of her duffel coat. Small in stature but large in personality, the Peke inevitably flagged after playing in the park with the bigger dogs.

She turned her head in disbelief. The voice was the same, but with his jaw cleanly shaven and his head covered in a traditional headdress he looked different from earlier…not different enough to make her consider for one second responding to the command with anything other than a laugh of sheer disbelief.

Ignoring him, she set off, her jaw set, her knees getting less shaky as she strode down the crowded street, hood up, shoulders hunched and staring fixedly ahead. As she weaved her way around people, Eva muttered the occasional rueful sorry when she collided with someone.

While she continued to ignore the car that shadowed her she was aware that the window had rolled up, but it continued its relentless but leisurely pursuit. She kept up a pace that just stopped short of running.

Not a single person came to her aid.

Typical, she thought as a group of teenagers made some laughing comments. I could be kidnapped in broad daylight and nobody would lift a finger. Eva let out a relieved sigh as she approached a busy intersection; the light showed red for pedestrians and green for the lane of traffic that the limousine occupied.

Her relief was short-lived when, rather than proceed, the gleaming monster hugging the kerb came to a total halt beside her, oblivious to the cacophony of hooting horns.

Eva turned her head. This was utterly ridiculous. 'Go away!' she wailed above the horns.

The window rolled down.

'Why are you running away?'

Her chin went up a defiant notch. 'I am not running away. I'm going home.'

'Have you thought of taking regular exercise?' Karim asked, his eyes moving from her flushed cheeks to her heaving bosom.

'Have you thought of taking a hint?' she cut back sarcastically. 'And for your information there's nothing wrong with my fitness levels.' It was a shame that the same couldn't be said of her hormone levels. 'Even if I don't have a stomach like a washboard.' *Like you*, Eva thought as an inconvenient image of his lean, streamlined body flashed across her vision.

She blinked hard to banish the image and added defiantly, 'And I happen to think that people, especially men who are obsessed with their bodies, are narcissistic and boring!'

'So do I.'

She gave a contemptuous snort. 'Am I meant to believe that your six pack is natural?'

'I am flattered that my…*six pack* has occupied your thoughts, but actually I don't want to discuss my exercise regime.' He tilted his head back and heard himself say, 'I like your body.' What man wouldn't?

The low husky words had more effect on her breathing than the impromptu cardiovascular workout had. Eva was glad her face was already red as her heart attempted to climb into her throat.

'Get in, Eva,' he said, bored irritation in his voice and twin lines of dark colour etched across the crest of his chiselled cheekbones.

'Yeah,' yelled the man in the car behind, 'do us a favour, Eva—for pity's sake, get in!' The comment was endorsed by several more voices from inside cars.

The limousine door swung open in silent invitation.

Muttering, 'I know I'll regret this,' Eva threw her bag inside, deriving some satisfaction from the fact it hit him square in the chest before she followed it.

As the car pulled smoothly away from the kerb and into the now slowly moving traffic Eva maintained her grip on the door.

'You are planning to jump out, possibly?'

Eva ignored the sarcasm and gave up waiting for her breathing to return to normal, finally accepting it wasn't going to happen while she was in an enclosed space that amplified the testosterone-fuelled-aura thing her travelling companion radiated like a force field.

The car was so ridiculously big that there was no question of anything uncomfortable like touching thighs.

Not that he looked as if he wanted to touch her—strangle her, possibly…? Back rigid, she turned her head slowly, willing her expression to stay neutral. 'If you have something to say, say it. I want to go home.'

'That might not be possible.'

Karim saw the flicker of uncertainty in her eyes, but a moment later she tilted her chin to a challenging angle. He fought off an unexpected stab of admiration. The lost princess might have a red-headed, bloody-minded attitude, but she also had spirit.

'Is that meant to scare me?' she jeered. 'What is this?' she added when a newspaper was placed unceremoniously on her lap.

She swallowed, conscious of the shiver of apprehension trickling like ice down her spine as her eyes flickered across the headline. Two phrases leapt out at her: VIRGIN PRINCESS and NIGHT OF PASSION.

She closed her eyes and thought, *Let me die.*

'Tomorrow's tabloid—it gets better inside,' he promised.

'Tomorrow's…?' Hope flared—did that mean there was still time to kill the story?

'Read it,' he suggested, watching the emotions flicker across her face. 'It will save explanations.'

'I've seen enough. I already feel sick. They can't write this sort of stuff, can they? Not once you tell them it's all lies.'

A spasm of irritation contorted his lean features as he leaned back in his seat. 'The editor gave it to me as a courtesy, so he said, but it was clear he was hoping for a quote. Why would I give him one?'

Eva pursed her lips and slung him a furious glare. 'So you didn't tell him it was all lies?'

He expelled a sigh through clenched teeth, muttered something in his native tongue and bowed his head before retorting, 'It is one version of the truth and, frankly, a lot more believable than yours.'

Eva didn't want to, but the lurid headline exerted a sick fascination and she found herself scanning it once more.

It did not read better the second time around… 'I feel sick.'

'*Feeling* I can cope with. Do us both a favour, though, and control your gag reflex.'

This heartless response drew a narrow-eyed glare from Eva. 'How did they get this?' she choked, shaking her head in utter mystification.

'From your reaction I'm assuming I can discount the possibility you are the source.'

Eva was not conscious she had raised her hand until he caught her wrist and leaned into her. The action was a signal for every nerve in her body to go haywire.

'Bad idea.' The unmistakable warning in his steely eyes belied the lightness in his tone.

Eva twisted her wrist and to her intense relief his fingers unfolded and his hand fell. She sat there, rubbing her wrist. 'You actually thought that I would…?'

'It was a possibility, but your friend was always the obvious candidate.'

'Luke!' she exclaimed. 'He would never betray…'

'You would be surprised how often people will betray you when there is a cheque involved…and sometimes,' he added, dragging his hair back from his broad brow with a hand, 'it doesn't even take a cheque.' In his experience revenge for an imagined slight was often enough.

Eva began to shake her head in instinctive rejection of the cynical interruption. Was he born this distrustful or had life made him this way?

'Luke is the least avaricious person I know. He definitely wouldn't…' She stopped, recalling how he became very willing to confide his life history to total strangers after a beer or two.

Reading the sudden flicker of doubt in her face, Karim shrugged. 'Or maybe he would?' he suggested.

Eva lifted her eyes, her lips thinned in distaste as she glared at him. At that moment she would have given a lot to be able to wipe that smug look off his face.

'It's possible the information leaked through Luke,' she conceded, able easily to imagine the scene. 'But he didn't do it deliberately and he *definitely* didn't do it for money.' She shook her head and added firmly, 'He wouldn't.'

Karim, whose initial strong dislike of the blond man had not faded in the last few hours, observed with a sceptical sneer, 'You have a lot of faith in your boyfriend.'

It contrasted strongly with her determination to assign the worst possible motives to his own actions.

'He is not my boyfriend,' Eva said, even though she didn't think her denial would have any more effect on his opinion now than it had on the previous occasion.

'So you do not have an exclusive relationship, but you have been together for…?'

'I've known Luke for some time and he's not…' She stopped and threw up her hands in frustration. 'What is it—don't you think a man and woman can be platonic friends?'

'No.'

'Just because you look on women as sex objects…' Eva gave a contemptuous sniff and promptly lost the thread of her argument as her glance drifted across the strong contours of his amazing face.

'Friendship between…' Her voice trailed away to nothing as she recognised the powerful sensuality carved into every perfect line, every plane and hollow of his face. Some women might not consider it a trial to have him consider them as sex objects…actually quite a lot of women.

He shrugged. 'I do not pretend to be a *modern man*.'

Her laugh almost tipped over into hysterical, but it did help break the spell that had her in its grip.

'You're a throwback to the Dark Ages.'

'And that is a bad thing? If you have any doubt turn to page eight. I believe the multiple-choice quiz there will tell you whether you are turned on by a sensitive contemporary man in touch with his female side or if you are one of that number who is drawn towards the masterful macho lover—in the "treat them mean keep them keen" vein.'

'Very funny,' she began, then stopped, adding in a hoarse horror-struck whisper, 'Page eight…there's more inside?'

'Oh, yes, quite a lot more. I'm especially fond of the insight-ful little piece on page five....'

Eva flicked through the pages and went paper-white. 'This is not funny!'

The anonymity that had allowed her to take up her old life had gone—the consequences would be a lot more serious now than bodyguards watching her flat.

Karim's mobile lips twisted into a grimace of angry distaste. 'You think I enjoy having my personal life made gossip fod-der?'

Eva realised for the first time that the mocking repartee hid an underlying anger... More than anger, she corrected, study-ing his face. Karim was incandescent with rage.

'This is your fault!' she accused as panic clutched like an icy fist in her belly.

'On what do you base that charge?'

'I'm ordinary—people do not write about me in tabloids. Is this even genuine?'

'Your lack of realism is beginning to irritate,' he observed. 'Your father was a prince, you are part of a powerful family, your actions have consequences and you did not spend the night with just anybody, you spent it with me.'

'You have to do something to stop them printing it!'

'There is such a thing as a free press.'

Until now Eva had always thought this was a good thing. 'It's all a lie!'

The plaintive cry elicited an unexpected twinge of sympathy from Karim. He ignored it; sympathy was not what she needed.

She needed to wake up.

'You think that makes any difference?'

'Of course it makes a difference.'

'Do not be so naïve!' Karim, his expression contemptuous, studied her indignant features.

'I'm not naïve!' A hopeful look appeared on her face. 'What about an...injunction?'

'A good idea,' he conceded. 'If what they had printed was not essentially true.'

'True!' she yelped. 'It's total rubbish!' She opened the paper with a rustle and found a headline. 'Right,' she said, stabbing it with her finger. 'For a start I'm not a—'

'Virgin, true,' he said, picking up on a totally different aspect. 'The virgin princess stuff makes a good headline, but as I imagine every lover you have ever had will be coming out of the woodwork to contradict that in rival papers, demanding a retraction would be pointless. Do you not think,' he added grimly, 'I would kill this story if I could? It is not in my power to do so—believing the world is the place you wish it to be does not make it so. Your grandfather hoped that you would gradually accept that your life had to change. He clearly underestimated your stubbornness.' His mouth lifted briefly in a humourless smile as he added half to himself, 'Or possibly overestimated your intelligence…?'

Eva's eyes flashed, but before she could respond to the insult he added, 'He now accepts that it was a mistake.'

'You have been discussing me with my grandfather? How dare you!'

'The announcement of our marriage will appear in the relevant places tomorrow.'

The autocratic pronouncement took Eva's breath away. It was unbelievable but he really seemed to think she would agree. 'And I have no say in this?' she asked, adopting an interested tone.

He shrugged and, leaning back into his seat, closed his eyes. 'Not a lot. Now, if you don't mind, I have things to do.'

Eva ground her teeth and fixed the impossible man with a glimmering glare. Did he really think that she was going to sit still for this manipulation?

'I do mind.' If he actually fell asleep she would kill him, she really would… Now that, she thought longingly, would *really* make a headline worth reading. 'Let me tell you…'

Karim opened his eyes. 'No, let *me* tell *you*, Princess,' he said with the manner of a man who had exhausted his patience, 'or better still let me show you…' This alternative would be admittedly brutal, but effective.

'Show?' she echoed, unable to understand a word of what he said to the man sitting up front in the driver's seat. 'What are you doing? What did you say to him? Stop this car immediately!' she added, tugging at the door handle, which didn't budge.

Eva, fighting the rising tide of panic, turned her head sharply, causing her hair to whip around her face as she faced him. 'You do know we have a law in this country about kidnap?'

As she studied his profile with angry eyes her expression grew abstracted; he looked like a man who made his own laws.

Which was, she reminded herself, *not* an admirable quality. Fitting her scowl back in place, she grumbled crankily, 'Just what sort of world would it be if we *all* went around making up the rules as we went along?'

It would be chaos…much as her life was at the moment. She was suddenly filled with a nostalgic longing for a time when she was oblivious to the existence of her exotic relations and the only prince she knew existed in the pages of books and magazines!

The blacked-out glass panel that separated them from the two men in the front of the car was back in place before Karim responded.

'You want to get out, fine…feel free.'

She tilted her head to look at him with confused suspicion. *'What?'*

'I'm not kidnapping you, I'm rescuing you, Princess,' he murmured softly.

'I do not need rescuing.' Not until now, anyway, she thought as his platinum eyes captured her own. 'And I'm not a princess.'

'You really do struggle with reality, don't you, Princess?'

The throbbing ache between her thighs was real and utterly

mortifying. 'This is not real.' Any minute now she would wake up, and she would not be lying in anyone's arms.

'This is a theme I have already touched on, but as you are clearly a slow learner I will repeat myself... Saying something, even with shrill conviction, does not make it so, Princess.'

Eva lifted a hand to cover the base of her throat, where she was conscious of a pulse frantically leaping.

'Do not call me that...and I'm not shrill.' Shrill would have been an improvement on breathy. The longer his eyes held hers, the stronger a hold the languid lethargy that had invaded her limbs became.

She disliked the entire out-of-control floaty feeling almost as much as the man who had caused it...without even trying.

What if he tried?

This horrifying thought made the idea of flinging herself from the moving vehicle not seem totally crazy and actually, the longer she considered it, the better an idea it became.

'Take me home!' She clenched her jaw against a grimace, shocked by the undercurrent of desperation in her shrill demand. 'I...' The rest of the words were lost when, without warning, he leant across her.

She froze, stopped breathing, stopped thinking, but carried on *feeling*... The sensual input was painful. His dark head was close enough for Eva to smell the scent of his shampoo, close enough for her to feel the heat of his body.

The moment did not last, but it was long enough for a drugged lethargy to wash over her and invade her limbs, then the door opened.

Eva didn't move. She looked at her avenue of escape blankly and felt her stomach dip as she thought about the tensile strength in the arm that brushed against her breasts.

He was no longer touching her, but she was even more painfully aware of the tingling sensation in her nipples and the mortifying gush of liquid heat low in her belly.

He was all hard bone and muscle, raw and male...

Her delicate blue-veined eyelids fluttered, her lashes quivering against her flushed cheeks before they lifted and their glances locked.

'You should not fight it. Marriage does not have to change everything… You and I have been enjoying empty sex outside marriage. I see no reason that we cannot carry on doing the same within marriage.'

The cynical observation hit her like a blast of cold air.

'You make it sound so tempting.'

'Your alternative, Eva, is there.'

Eva followed the direction of his nod and looked out into the scene framed by the open door and discovered the car had pulled over at the end of the road where she lived.

A peaceful, quiet backwater, that at that moment was neither peaceful nor quiet. She blinked, trying to make sense of what she was seeing. Had there been an accident…a gas leak?

It had to be something pretty serious to bring TV crews with cameras here.

'You wanted to go home.'

'I don't understand what's happened.'

'We have happened.'

'Oh, my God!'

It was hard to hear her horrified whisper and not feel a pang of sympathy, but the emotion did not show in his manner as Karim asked, 'You still want to go home?'

Eva continued to stare in utter bewilderment at the people, too many to count, milling around at the far end of the street. 'But where did they all come from? Why…?'

'Why do you think?'

Eva, conscious of an icy fist of dread in her belly, felt panic lodged like a boulder behind her breastbone. 'Me…?' she said, losing all colour.

'A student, the daughter of a famous man-hater, who didn't know who her father was, let alone that he was a prince…

Even if you had no connection with me this story would run and run…'

'But they'll lose interest. I'm just—'

'The numbers will have doubled by morning.'

The brutal observation made her flinch. 'But when will I be able to go home?'

'Do I have to spell it out? Every nut job in the country knows where you live. Pictures of you looking cute in pigtails and braces will be on TV screens. People who are your closest friends will tell their warts-and-all stories, lovers you have forgotten existed will crawl out of the woodwork.'

'There are no…' She stopped, closed her eyes and pressed a clenched fist to her mouth. The realisation hit her with the force of a boulder landing on her chest—life as she knew it was over.

She felt resentment rise like bile inside her, and opened her angry green eyes. On one level she knew it was utterly irrational to lay the blame for all this at the feet of Karim, but she needed someone to blame and his shoulders were broad.

Her accusing gaze drifted downwards and she thought, Very broad, while struggling to ignore the mental image of him without a shirt.

CHAPTER SEVEN

'THANK you so much for putting a positive spin on the situation,' Eva said, injecting silky calm into her voice as she dragged her eyes from the almost surreal scene in the street to Karim's face.

She surprised a look on his face that had he been anyone else at all she would have interpreted as sympathy.

'If you want positive spin or, for that matter, *spin*, I'm not your man.'

'You're not my man,' she retorted seamlessly.

'I could be.'

'I…' Her protective anger fell away so abruptly that Eva shivered. The anger had been her insulation, her protection. Suddenly she felt exposed, vulnerable and more alone than she had in her life previously.

She reached for his hand and held on as if he were the only thing between her and drowning.

'I can't go home, can I? Not ever.'

It wasn't a question.

She heard the choked sound of distress that came from her throat and bit down hard on her quivering lip, determined not to give him the satisfaction of falling apart before his eyes.

'It is rarely a good thing to go backwards, or even stand still.'

His voice was almost unrecognisably gentle… She sniffed and clung to his hand. Was he trying to make her cry?

Karim struggled to maintain his objectivity as he watched her struggle to come to terms with reality. It was a big task… this sort of thing was tough enough if you had been brought up knowing that your every thoughtless action and careless word would be seized on by the media, scrutinised and pored over.

Karim hardened his heart and reminded himself that she was overdue a reality check.

A cry from outside made Eva turn.

'It's her!'

Someone took up the cry and all turned in their direction. She watched as the pack began to advance en masse towards them.

Karim spoke to the driver in his native tongue and, leaning across her, pulled the door closed, shutting out the yells and the crowds. 'It's all right.' His hand went to the back of her head as she leaned into his chest; she was shaking hard.

'I can't do this.' Her hands clenched into her sides, her nails gouging half moons into the soft flesh of her palms as she fought back the sobs of emotion that rose in her throat.

'I can.'

It was no boast, just a statement of fact.

She turned her head. In profile his features radiated confidence and maybe some of it seeped into her because she was able to control the quiver in her voice as she asked, 'So what happens now?' *Don't think too far ahead*, she advised herself— *just take things one step at a time*. 'Do I have to go into hiding or something?' Her smile was painfully false as she added, 'Should I dye my hair and wear dark glasses?'

Her comment drew Karim's glance to her bright head and an image of it lying spread out on a pillow around her face flashed into his head. His jaw tightened.

'That should not be necessary.' But it might be necessary to put his libido back in its box; he had no time for distractions while he had this many potentially explosive balls in the air.

Eva shrugged. 'Just an idea. So what does happen now?'

Feeling emotionally battered, she struggled to feel any real interest in his response.

'We are going to the hospital.' As he turned his head to assess her reaction to this information it occurred to Karim that had he walked through the doors of Casualty with Eva now they would have jumped her to the head of the queue.

The only trace of colour in her alabaster-pale face was the deep emerald green of her spectacular eyes. Her pallor served to emphasise the impression of fragility suggested by her fine-boned features and slight build.

Her self-possessed act might be more convincing if she had been able to stop her teeth audibly chattering.

'A hospital?'

He nodded.

'Why—are you ill?' There was still the suggestion of shadows of fatigue under his eyes, but he was projecting an aura of such vitality that Eva struggled to associate it as a sign of physical vulnerabilty.

'I am not,' he confirmed. 'But my daughter is.'

Her eyes widened. 'You have a daughter?' Eva didn't know why the information came as such a shock.

His brows lifted. 'Is there any reason I should not have a daughter?'

The regal hauteur in his manner made her feel irrationally defensive. 'No, that is...no reason at all. I just didn't...' She stopped and angled him a questioning look. 'She's not well?'

'No.'

The words *'blood out of a stone'* popped into Eva's head as she regarded him with growing frustration. 'I'm sorry your daughter isn't well.' And it would explain why resolving her problem was less of a priority. Eva realised that she had been relying too heavily on the hope he could pluck a solution out of the air.

This was her problem, she reminded herself.

'Your wife.'

'She died.'

'Sorry,' she said, wincing at the inadequacy.

Able to hear the *next* probing question she was working towards, he acknowledged her words with a curt jerk of his head and said, 'We were married nearly seven years. She was killed in a car accident two years ago. I have had lovers since.' He arched a brow. 'Does that satisfy your curiosity?'

Eva looked away and thought, Not really. He hadn't answered the important questions like had he loved his wife? Did he still love her?

Karim regretted his tone. He was aware that, as the only person available, she was taking the brunt of his growing tension. The final round of blood results would be revealed soon. He was trying hard not to anticipate them one way or the other, and failing.

It actually helped being forced to turn his thoughts to something that he could control—he slid a glance towards the woman beside him and thought, To a degree.

Eva registered that they were entering an underground car park, a vast echoing concrete space. If this was for the hospital, business was not good because they were literally the only vehicle in it.

'If you want to visit, I'll wait in the car. Don't worry, I'll duck down if anyone comes,' she promised.

'I admire your ingenuity but there will be no other cars.'

Before she could question this peculiar prediction he added, 'And you are coming with me.'

Eva threw him a doubtful look. 'If your daughter is ill she might not want to see strangers.'

'I will visit my daughter alone after the ceremony.'

All at sea now, Eva shook her head. 'What ceremony?'

'The civil wedding ceremony. By the time the story appears we will be husband and wife.'

Eva stared. 'You know, you don't look insane.'

'Of course, the venue is not ideal.'

The concession drew a strangled laugh from Eva.

'King Hassan favoured waiting until he arrives tomorrow, but—'

Eva's eyes shot wide. 'My grandfather is coming...?' she yelped in alarm. 'What is this—a conspiracy?' Stupid question— of course it was.

He ignored her interruption and said calmly, 'We met when at your grandfather's palace last year.'

'We did?' she said, humouring him.

'Yes.'

'And was it love at first sight?'

Frowning at her sarcastic interjection, he continued stonily, 'The official wedding plans were put on hold when Amira became ill. But we married in secret at a civil ceremony because you wished to be by my side and support me through this difficult time.'

Eva found it bizarre to hear this fairy story recounted in a flat, detached tone she associated with someone reciting the periodic table.

'And this is your idea of a solution?' She shook her head. 'You look like you have a mind like a steel trap—how wrong could I be? I won't even bother pointing out all the flaws in your plan, because it isn't going to happen.'

'That is up to you.'

'That's the first sane thing you've said,' Eva observed, feeling not at all comforted by his admission.

'Look, I don't have the time for this.' He glanced down at the watch on his wrist and the furrow lines between his brows deepened. 'So I will spell out the facts and then you may make your decision.'

She shook her head. 'It doesn't matter what you say—' She intercepted his expression and, with a disgruntled sniff, said, 'Oh, all right, then, I'm listening.'

'Your grandfather is a pragmatic man. He is not averse to change and progress, but he understands that such things are not brought about overnight. He could impose change but he would not because he knows that for change to succeed he must take his people with him on the journey.'

He said her grandfather but as she listened Eva got the impression that the philosophy he espoused was perhaps a little more personal—his own?

'Honour seems an old-fashioned concept to you.'

He was presuming she had no moral values; Eva's lips tightened at the assumption.

'But,' he continued, 'it is a central precept to your grandfather's life. If King Hassan did not react to an insult offered his granddaughter he would lose respect and be viewed as a weak king. He has no choice in this matter.'

'Is he very angry?' she asked in a small voice.

'Not with you.'

'With you...' Her shoulders slumped. 'Oh, God! I'm sorry, I really am, but don't worry,' she added brightly. 'I'll make it right. I'll tell him how it was that you were...I'll—'

Looking visibly unappreciative of her assurance, Karim cut across her, his voice sounding to Eva awfully like that of a man who had reached the limit of his—*limited*—patience.

'Have you been listening to a word I have said? Clearly not.'

The dry afterthought brought a militant sparkle to her eyes. 'I can—'

'No,' he interrupted in a tone that made Eva retreat back into her seat. 'You do not appear to understand anything. If this scandal is not smothered before it takes on a life of its own—' Karim had seen it happen '—there will be consequences. Consequences that no earnest assurances or your version of the truth will alter.'

Eva's defiance in the face of his uncompromising edict was shaky. 'What could happen that would be so bad?'

Even as she voiced the perfectly valid question the voice in her head was saying, *Bad idea.*

The voice got louder when Karim smiled with, it seemed to

a resentful Eva, a certain grim relish and told her, 'The contract that is yet to be signed to allow the pipeline from our oilfields to pass through Azharim in order to reach the coast—this would not happen. The knock-on effect…' He shrugged.

'It would be massive and not just economic. This thing will not happen in isolation. The surrounding countries of the region would undoubtedly be drawn in—sides would be taken.

'Political stability is not something we take for granted. It is something we work at and have done for many years. Our countries have collaborated on several projects, at the present a cancer hospital—it would be the only one in the area.'

The light of determination in his eyes glowed bright as Karim considered the project that was very close to his own heart.

The royal connection went deep. His own cousin, Hakim, who was an internationally renown oncologist—Hakim had diagnosed Amira's condition—had left his position at a Swiss clinic to personally get the project up and running.

'So no pressure then.' Underneath her flippancy Eva was feeling utterly trapped; she felt as if the stability of an entire region had been placed on her shoulders.

He levelled a questioning look at her pale face and said quietly, 'You wish me to go on?'

Eva's disbelieving laugh contained no humour. 'There's more?'

Karim stayed silent and she turned her head, looking out of the window into the empty car park. 'I get the general idea. If I don't marry you, I'll be responsible for, well, just about anything and everything.' She expelled a shaky breath and gave another strained little laugh. 'I suppose it would be easier to say what I won't be responsible for.'

'It is your choice.'

It so was not! Eva, her eyes filled with simmering resentment, turned in her seat to face him. 'It's moral blackmail.'

'It is necessity, but semantics aside—'

'Semantics aside,' she gritted though clenched teeth, 'you're relying heavily on me having a conscience.'

A glimmer of emotion Eva struggled to put a name to flickered across his face before he took her chin between his finger and tilted her face up to his.

'I *know* you have a conscience, so, yes, this is a stacked deck, but remember I am not asking you to do something that I am not willing to do myself.'

His fingers slipped away and Eva, her full lower lip caught between her teeth, dropped her gaze and didn't see Karim's shoulders relax in relief when she nodded her head.

'I feel like I've just jumped off a cliff.' *And while I'm doing it all I can think about is the texture of his skin...which makes me not only suicidal, but insane!*

'Don't worry. As your husband it will be my job to catch you.'

'Oh, don't worry—if I jump I'll take you with me.'

A slow smile spread across his sombre features. 'A woman who thinks in terms of retribution...I can identify with that.'

Eva closed her eyes; she was so out of her depth!

The lift doors opened onto a large square reception area.

It was ultra-modern and like no hospital Eva had ever seen. The decor involved a great deal of glass. Staring at a solid wall of it with water running over it, Eva followed Karim's impatient direction to precede him.

The two men who had ridden up with them in the lift stayed there as the doors slid silently closed and another older man also clad in similar robes materialized, it seemed to a bemused Eva, out of thin air.

He bowed low to them both—Eva always found that embarrassing—and spoke to Karim in Arabic.

Karim said little, but nodded several times as though what the other man had said satisfied him. Eva had the impression that he'd have said if it didn't.

Karim did not strike her as a man who would tolerate incompetence in silence, or it seemed, if his expression when she spoke was any indicator, a bride-to-be who spoke out of turn.

'This is a hospital?'

His eyes briefly brushed her face. 'Yes, this is a hospital.' He then proceeded to ignore her and turn back to the other man.

'How are you going to keep this under wraps? Won't someone see us?' she suggested, seeing a gaping hole in this plan.

Eva wasn't sure if it was the question or the interruption that caused a spasm of irritation to cross Karim's lean features.

'If you are hoping for a last-minute reprieve—don't,' he advised. 'Do you see people?' His nod took in the empty places behind a large reception desk. 'Do you see anyone?'

She shook her head. The place was deserted.

'No, and you will not. Tariq—' he nodded towards the older man '—has cleared our route.'

The man under discussion nodded respectfully to her and spoke into his earpiece before confirming calmly in English, 'The route has been cleared.'

Eva stared. 'But how…?'

It was Karim who replied. 'A lot of things are possible when one is donating a new clinic.' If these people saved Amira he would donate a new hospital!

'I suppose it is,' she said faintly.

'Then come,' Karim urged. 'I want to get this over with.'

A strangled laugh was drawn from Eva's aching throat. 'And they say romance is dead.'

'You want romance?'

Smothering her growing desire to say, Wake me when this is over, she met his eyes; they were as cold as ice. 'No, I don't.' Could this day get any more surreal?

'Fine, then let us…'

The tall man that Karim had called Tariq cleared his throat and bowed his head to Eva. 'I thought these might be appropriate,' he said, producing a large bouquet like a magician.

Karim fought his impatience; his conference with the medical team taking care of Amira was in ten minutes' time. 'That is hardly necessary—'

'Not necessary, but very thoughtful,' Eva interrupted, accepting the flowers and smiling her gratitude to the man with the stony face. The look she cast Karim held less warmth.

Karim told himself that Tariq was welcome to her smiles and gritted his teeth. 'Fine, have the flowers.'

'I will!' Eva retorted, holding the sweet-smelling posy to her chest as she scowled defiantly up at him.

She was doing what he wanted; she was jumping through all the hoops; she was signing her life away—would it really hurt him, she wondered bitterly, to be civil at least?

'Come!' Karim reached out, but before he could grab her arm he released a shocked cry of pain.

'Oh, no, I'd forgotten.' Eva grabbed the furry bundle that was attached by its teeth to Karim's wrist and, tapping its nose, pushed it back into her pocket, where she assumed it had been asleep.

The rock-faced man did the spooky magician thing again and produced a clean white bandage and Karim began it wrap to around his wrist.

'What is that thing in your pocket?'

Eva shook her head mutely. He looked pretty mad—considering the blood on the floor, possibly, she conceded, with some justification.

'I take it *you* did not growl or bite me?'

Neither seemed such a bad idea to Eva. 'You scared her,' she said defensively. 'She must have fallen asleep.'

'What is it?'

'A dog, obviously.'

Karim's brows lifted. It looked like no dog he had ever seen. 'It looked like a rodent.'

'Why would I be carrying a *rodent* around in my pocket?'

He lifted his eyebrows and she flushed. 'I told you I walk

dogs, and I forgot she was there.' She had delivered all but Sukie safely back to their owners when she had been plucked from the street.

'Walk? The creature was in your pocket? Or does it get its exercise biting innocent passers-by?'

Her eyes skimmed his mouth. 'You're not innocent, and I only put her in my pocket when she's tired.' Frolicking around the park with a bunch of long-legged dogs tired out the little creature. 'And it was raining. She's not keen on water.'

Karim's expression showed pretty clearly what he thought of a water-hating dog. He turned to Tariq, who had again anticipated his needs.

'Zadik will look after the animal,' he said, indicating a younger man who appeared slightly breathless beside them.

'Hand it over, Eva.'

Eva's mutinous expression revealed her reluctance to comply. 'She's a pedigree and worth a lot. You won't—'

'Eat it?' Karim snapped. He imagined a long-distance runner with the winning line in sight might feel the way he did if the endline was constantly moving.

Unable to contain his impatience another second, he took matters into his own hands in the literal sense and, reaching into her pocket, removed the ball of fluff that growled low in its throat.

He handed it to the bowing younger man. 'Dog has been off our menus for some years now. Enough of this…come…' He extended his hand and, after a moment's heart-thudding hesitation, Eva put her own into it.

Her feelings when his brown fingers closed over hers were disturbingly ambiguous.

Led down the corridors that were, as promised, totally empty, she was aware of the silent presence of several robed figures all sporting earpieces like Tariq and all looking ready for anything.

They stopped outside a door that looked no different from

any other they had passed, and after opening it Tariq bowed and stood to one side to allow them to enter before him.

Eva, shaking her head, pulled her hand from Karim's.

'I can't get married in a duffel coat.' Even if it was a damage-limitation exercise more than a marriage.

Karim shot her a look that brimmed with impatience. 'Then take it off.' The advice just stopped short of a snarl.

'Allow me, Princess.'

Eva turned, surprised to find herself directly addressed by Tariq, who, after bowing gently, eased the heavy coat off her shoulders.

'Thank you,' she said uncertainly.

Inside her head a voice was saying, *Run...run...* but her feet were moving in the wrong direction with the help of an encouraging smile from the older man and Karim's firm hand in the small of her back.

Clutching her flowers, Eva heard the doors close with a click of finality behind her and felt a strange sense of calm wash over her. The calm lasted throughout the brief ceremony.

It was a feeling similar to being in a dream and knowing it and relaxing because you knew that it didn't matter what happened because you were going to wake up.

It wasn't until a few minutes later, when she was standing outside in the corridor with a ring on her finger and Karim totally ignoring her while he conversed in a mixture of French and Arabic to Tariq, that she realised she wasn't going to wake up. This was real; she was married.

She had woken from a dream and found herself in the middle of a nightmare. The calm that had supported her vaporised and icy panic slid in to fill the space it left. It clogged her throat and filled her churning stomach.

What had she done?

'Go with Tariq.'

Eva bit her trembling lip and tilted her face to his; the man she had married looked remote and stern.

'But…you…?'

'I need to be with Amira.' Mentally, Eva realized, he already was; he was looking right through her.

'Can I do anything…help…?'

'You?'

Eva swallowed, trying hard not to show how much the rejection hurt. Her response was, she knew, irrational, but she had no control over it.

'I just thought…'

'If you want to help go with Tariq. He will take care of you.' He nodded once more in her direction and strode away.

Eva watched the tall, elegant figure until he vanished from view. She turned her head and caught an expression of sympathy on the face of the man beside her.

The idea that she was an object of pity for members of Karim's household filled her with horror. She immediately pinned on a cheery smile.

'So what next?'

'I will escort you to—'

Unable to maintain the pretence of listening, Eva, her voice tense, cut across him. 'Is she very ill?'

There was a pause before Tariq, looking uncomfortable at being directly addressed, responded, 'Yes, she is.'

'And he…Prince Karim…he has spent a lot of time here?'

'He has barely left her side.'

'And that is where he is now?'

'The doctors have been trying some experimental treatment. They will be able to tell the Prince today if it is working.' He stopped and looked as though he regretted revealing so much, then, bowing his head, he gestured for her to precede him. 'If you would come this way, the Prince has asked me to—'

Eva began to move, then stopped. 'He's alone—I mean, there's no family or anything with him?'

'No, he is alone.'

Eva narrowed her eyes and took a deep breath. 'No.' Smiling

with a confidence she was not feeling—she was not in the habit of blindly following her instinct—she turned to face the tall, forbidding figure beside her.

She might be a wife in name only, but the thought of Karim facing what could be bad news…the *worst* news…alone just seemed so wrong.

It was totally irrational, but she felt she *should* be there. He might not want a shoulder to cry on, especially hers, but she'd be someone to yell at if nothing else.

'Sorry, Princess, I don't quite understand…'

'No.'

A wary light appeared in Tariq's dark eyes.

'The Prince has asked you to keep me out of his hair.' She arched a brow. 'Am I right?'

Tariq, looking nonplussed by the comment, let his arm fall back to his side. 'The Prince is anxious that you are comfortable, that you have what you wish.'

'I wish to see him.' He might not want to see me.

'I'm afraid that that will not—'

'Look, I'm not sure what your job description covers, but I'm pretty sure it doesn't include manhandling a royal princess, and that's the only way you're moving me from here.'

She held her breath, not totally sure what she'd do if he called her bluff.

She thought she saw the glimmer of a smile in his eyes as he inclined his head and said, 'This way.'

The room that Tariq showed her to was on the top floor. He spoke to the two men who stood outside and they bowed and stepped aside.

She gave them a smile as she walked past, thinking, *What are you doing, Eva? The man doesn't need you. He is more than capable of looking after himself. He'll just think you're interfering.*

On the threshold she paused uncertainly, bracing herself for Karim's reaction when he saw her.

He didn't react because he didn't see her. Her glance moved from the tiny waxy-faced figure in the bed, so slight that her arm seemed too fragile to hold all the tubes that protruded from it, to the tall man standing by the window looking blindly out at the city below.

She saw the moisture on his cheeks and empathy so acute it hurt swelled in her chest.

Her heart aching for his grief, she moved towards him, her hand outstretched. 'I'm so sorry, Karim.'

At the sound of her voice he turned his head. 'Eva?'

She saw then that it was not grief and pain that shone in his eyes, but joy and relief.

Her hand fell away self-consciously. 'I'm sorry, I didn't mean to intrude but—'

'It is working,' he said, his eyes on the figure in the bed. 'She's going to be all right.'

The expression on his face as he looked at his daughter brought a lump to her throat. 'I'm so glad, Karim,' she said softly.

'You're here?' he said as if just registering her presence.

Feeling like an intruder, she absently rubbed her fingers across the ring on her left hand and nodded. 'I just thought I might be able to do something to help, but I can see—'

'You want to help?' he said, his voice low and gravelly.

Unable to read his expression as he advanced with panther-like grace towards her, Eva shook her head. 'It was just a thought.'

He stopped just in front of her. The tension she could feel rolling off him in waves made her senses spin. His deep-set eyes glittered as he looked down at her. 'You can help.'

'I…'

He hooked a finger under her chin, growling, 'Don't talk.' And brought his mouth down hard on hers.

Her shocked gasp was lost in his mouth as her lips parted under the sensuous pressure. She had not known a kiss could be like this: raw, possessive, passionate and hungry. Molten heat seared her nerve endings as she melted into him with a sigh and kissed him back, sliding her fingers deep into his hair and groaning at the first stabbing intrusion of his tongue inside her mouth.

When he finally lifted his head they were both breathing hard. 'Oh!' She sighed, unpeeling her arms from his neck as he placed her back on her feet.

'Indeed!'

'Did that help?' she whispered, staring at him with starry stunned eyes. She could still taste him in her mouth.

The voice in her head warned she was wildly overreacting to a kiss that had obviously been an outward release of his tension, but she couldn't help it.

If that was him using her, she couldn't wait for him to do it again.

'It hurt.' Dragging his mouth from hers had been one of the hardest things he had ever done. 'It hurt to stop...' he clarified in response to her bewildered expression.

'Oh!'

He studied her flushed face. 'You look like a girl who has never been kissed before.'

Never like that, she thought, unable to think of a single thing to say that wouldn't come out as, Please do it again.

Eva cleared her throat. 'It was unexpected.' She wanted him so badly her bones ached with it. The intensity of what she was feeling simultaneously shocked and excited her. 'Like getting married,' she observed with a nervous laugh. 'I was thinking more along the lines of a cup of tea or a sandwich.'

'You taste better than a sandwich.'

The smouldering heat in his eyes sent a fresh pulse of longing through her body. 'So do you.'

'I think it might be a good idea if you went with Tariq now.'

She felt a stab of hurt that fell away as he added, 'This is not the place or time for us to continue this…*conversation.*'

The frustrated glow in his eyes was a soothing balm to her ego. 'You're staying?'

'Amira wakes in the night and the nurses struggle to settle her.' Karim pulled a chair across to his daughter's bedside and lowered himself into it. 'Love for a child is something that tears your heart out.' He slid a sideways glance towards Eva as he added softly, 'When you have children of your own you will understand.'

Eva blinked at the comment. 'I hadn't thought about children.'

His frown made her realise it might have been an idea to censor her response. 'Well, think about it now, Princess, because I am duty-bound to provide an heir.'

Eva tensed as the word *duty* sent a chill through her body. She shivered; it sounded so clinical.

'An heir?' she echoed.

'There has been impatience in some quarters. The news I am married will be greeted with a sigh of relief.'

'You expect me to have your children?' She looked at him in horror.

A nerve clenched along his jaw. 'Whose children did you expect to have?' he asked, seeing the handsome blond academic.

'No one's…that is, children are meant to be the result of love, not…'

'Empty sex?' he suggested, not quite sure why her reaction made him so angry, but totally sure she was in the wrong. 'Are you looking for love, Eva?'

She flushed and bit her quivering lip. 'No, I'm not.'

Liar, he thought, looking at her face and not wanting to stop. 'Let it stay that way. I don't want you falling for me,' he warned. 'I'm not into needy women.'

He could be very cruel. She wondered about the first wife

who had given him the daughter he clearly adored, presumably he had loved her. Maybe he still did?

She lowered her eyes and struggled to lower the emotional temperature.

It hardly boded well—married literally five minutes and they were already fighting. And she had no idea how or why— it had just sort of exploded like the sexual chemistry that had preceded it. 'Like you said, this isn't the right time for this conversation.'

Karim scowled. He knew that this was not the right time but all he could see was the horror on her face at the suggestion she have his children. 'Contrary to your belief, *empty* sex produces children just as efficiently as true love, which is as well for us.

'And don't act as though it would be a hardship, because I just kissed you and you didn't want me to stop. For some people empty sex is all there is and so far we've both been enjoying it with other people. The only change is we start enjoying it with each other.'

Eva went paper white. 'I don't want sex with you, empty or otherwise, and if I were you I'd invest in a good self-help book. They probably have an entire chapter on men who have to precede *sex* with *empty*!'

Karim gave a thin-lipped smile. 'You want it so badly you can taste it…' His voice trailed off as he looked at her and felt need flood through his body. He had never needed a woman before…*wanted* but not *needed*.

It was suddenly very important to Karim to prove this had not changed, that what he was feeling now was a reaction to the weeks of stress and the sudden release of tension.

'You want me so badly that you'll beg me to take you.' At what point in this exchange had the connection between his brain and vocal cords become severed? Or had he regressed to his teenage years? wondered a deeply embarrassed Karim.

The words brought a rosy flush of outrage to Eva's cheeks,

but she was too mortified to register the thin strips of hot colour along his cheekbones. 'Never!' she choked.

'You'll—'

'I'm sorry, I didn't know.' The nurse standing in the doorway gave an apologetic smile. 'I can come back.'

Eva shook her head and forced a stiff smile. 'No, it's fine. I'm just going.'

The nurse glanced towards Karim and, in response to the almost imperceptible movement of his head, vanished in a swirl of efficient white.

Eva, who had watched the interplay, felt her temper spike. 'Lovely!' She flashed him a smile of fake sincerity and added grimly, 'I can look forward to a life of total invisibility.' She flashed the child in the bed a sideways look and struggled to contain her emotions as she began to back towards the door. Karim was right about one thing: this was not the place or time.

'I spoke in the heat of the moment...' Karim could hardly believe the childish taunt had come from his lips, but this woman somehow had the ability to goad him into rash actions and unconsidered words.

Eva stopped backing and stared, her breathing gradually slowing, as astonishment replaced anger. 'Did you just apologise?'

He gave a non-committal shrug that Eva interpreted as assent. 'So I don't have to beg?' Her eyes fell from his. It suddenly felt as if that was *exactly* what she was doing.

'You...' This time it was Karim's eyelashes that swept downwards, concealing his expression from a frustrated Eva.

'Well?' she prompted.

'You have been forced by circumstances to accept me as your husband, but it is clear you have not thought through the implications.'

Eva stared. 'When would I have been doing this deep thinking—on the way up in the lift?'

'Well, now I am giving you the time. You consider yourself sexually experienced…'

He raised a brow at the squeak that escaped her lips, but Eva shook her head and said in a choked whisper, 'Go on, this is fascinating.'

'If you come to my bed it will not be for one night or even two…there will be no other men.'

'So you're giving me the option of sleeping with you or taking lovers?'

'No!'

The violent explosive negative made Eva take an involuntary step backwards and the sleeping child in the bed mumbled and tossed restlessly.

His guilty glance swivelling towards his daughter, Karim clenched his jaw.

He struggled to compose his thoughts into some semblance of logic and order. One thing an arranged marriage had going for it was it made for a peaceful life—sterile but peaceful. No strong emotions, no jealousies and no passion to distract a man who had a country and people who needed him.

So what had gone wrong?

Amira's mother had taken lovers and he had not lost a moment's sleep over her discreet infidelities, so why did the thought of Eva's *hypothetical* lovers drive him close to losing control?

His angry eyes swept her upturned features. The impulse to tangle his fingers in her hair and draw her face to his was so strong that for the space of several seconds he could not breathe.

He did not need her. He *wanted* her.

The subtle differentiation made the torrent of emotions that had surfaced in him—emotions that he saw no reason to name—easier to file under 'unusual but not important'.

'There will be no lovers, and if you come to my bed you must accept that we will have children.' He spoke with a calm he was struggling to claim.

He had survived his disastrous first marriage emotionally intact because his first bride had awoken nothing that approached the primal hunger that tied his stomach into a frustrated knot, but it was just sex and he could and would stay in control.

A man who gave anything more than his body to a woman was asking to be stabbed in the back.

'So if I don't want a baby...I can't have you? No middle ground?'

His reply was about as uncompromising as his expression. 'No. You have to accept this is not an affair. This is marriage. I need to provide my country with an heir—therefore once you come to my bed there must be no one else.'

'You mean, when I get bored with sex with you I'll have to close my eyes and pretend you're...' Eva's comeback faltered when she failed miserably to think of any man who did not look like a pale imitation when compared to the man she found herself married to.

She expected her belated silly addition of, 'Luke!' to produce a scornful laugh, but it didn't.

The lick of pure molten white outrage she glimpsed in his eyes before he pointedly turned his back on her made her realise that the only predictable thing about Karim was her ability to make him furious.

As she left the room his body language suggested he would not be following her any time soon.

CHAPTER EIGHT

HER grandfather stayed three days and during that time Eva was literally never alone with Karim.

He spent his days at the hospital, returned in the evening and dined with her grandfather. She was there but she might as well have been invisible for all the notice the men took of her.

The marriage seemed to have appeased her grandfather and the initial tension between the two men had rapidly thawed.

The same could not be said of the tension between Karim and her, but then it wasn't the same type of tension! Since that night in Amira's hospital room Karim had not attempted to touch her...but it was the *almost* occasions that were driving her slowly out of her mind.

Such as when he *almost* brushed her fingers with his when he passed her something, she got light-headed just anticipating the next time.

Sometimes even thinking about him touching her sent electrical thrills of sensation through her hopelessly receptive body.

The thought of what would happen when he did touch her for real scared her witless. He had put the ball in her court when he had spelt out what coming into his bed meant...it really was a 'burning the bridges' moment.

There was no mistaking that there was chemistry, and Eva, while still finding it amazing Karim was attracted to her, found it almost as amazing that she could want a man in this all-consuming way and not be in love with him.

The two had always been inextricably linked in her stubbornly romantic mind.

So *now* he wanted her, but Eva was under no illusion that this would last, and what about when his visits to her bed were made from a sense of duty? Her blood turned to ice at the thought of passion turning to something clinical and cold.

The whole thing seemed horribly inevitable.

It was on the last night of her grandfather's visit that it was announced that it had been decided she journey back with him and stay at the Palace in Azharim until Amira was fit enough to travel home with Karim.

Eva, who had sat quietly through the meal and was rapidly tiring of her invisible status, allowed her gaze to travel from one man to the other and back again.

'Decided by who exactly...? I didn't decide anything.'

King Hassan looked genuinely bewildered by the spiky comment. 'Surely you can have no objection to seeing your family...your cousins...?'

Eva forced herself to smile at her grandfather. 'I would just like to be consulted.'

'Consider yourself consulted,' Karim said, sounding bored by the entire subject. Amira's condition ought to be occupying his every waking moment, yet he was continually distracted by the hunger of his own body. Life would be simpler if the distraction was put out of temptations way for the moment at least.

And it wasn't just that it was the irrational guilt he was experiencing—he knew he had not trapped her into this marriage, that she had been equally culpable—but when he saw the dejected set of her shoulders he felt as though the responsibility was his.

'We are only thinking of you, Eva.'

That, Karim thought, keeping his eyes steadfastly on Eva's grandfather, is the problem.

'Karim has so much on his plate at the moment, with matters of state and Amira, he is worried that he will have no time to spend with you.'

Worried my foot, Eva thought, struggling to control her temper. He wants me out of his hair so that he can pick up with whatever bimbo he's sleeping with without worrying about his wife walking in.

Recognising the stab of jealousy that spilled like poison through her body, Eva went stiff with shock. She responded with defensive aggression.

'Surely Karim's father can deal with *matters of state*.'

It had crossed Eva's mind a couple of times recently to ask about Karim's father, but on each occasion she had been distracted, and now that she paused to think about it it seemed strange that he had never entered the equation.

Her grandfather's approval had been sought, but there had been no mention of what the King of Zuhaymi thought of his son's marriage.

An awkward silence followed her question.

It was Karim who broke it. 'My father no longer takes an active part in government.' His lashes came downwards concealing his expression from her as he speared a piece of food onto his fork. Then, not lifting it, he moved it around his plate.

'Why? He can't be that old?'

'Eva…' King Hassan began in a warning tone.

Karim lifted his head and said, 'No, she should know.'

'It may have escaped your notice, but actually I'm here in this room.'

'My father is not old, but he was diagnosed with early-onset Alzheimer's several years ago.'

It was still difficult to speak of recalling the first signs; watching such a robust virile man lose a part of himself everyday had been agonising.

'He does not appear in public any longer.' It made him feel guilty to acknowledge it, but there were times when Karim almost felt envious for those who had lost loved ones. It was, he had learnt, harder to grieve for the loss when that person or at least the shell was still alive.

'You mean, you locked him away when he became an embarrassment.'

When Karim met her accusing stare she saw, not the guilt she had anticipated in his face, but cold condemnation.

'When he was still able, he made it clear that once he was unable to function fully he wanted to retire from the public view. He lives today at a cottage beside the sea with a team of nurses to provide round-the-clock nursing. I see him but not as often as I would like because my presence sometimes agitates him.' The occasional flashes of lucidity when his father recognised him made the entire situation harder in many ways.

Eva could feel the heat of her grandfather's disapproval. Not that it made her feel any more wretched than she already did—nothing could.

'I'm sorry. That was a terrible thing to say to you and I'm very sorry about your father.'

Karim nodded his head and said, 'Apology accepted.' She wasn't sure if he meant it or if he was just going through the motions, but she felt even more of an outsider than ever.

'I'd like to go back to Azharim with you if the offer is still open.'

Her grandfather looked at her, concern in his eyes, and said, 'Of course it is.'

'Right,' she said, pushing her chair away from the table. 'I'll just go and pack.' She couldn't wait to escape the room and Karim's disapproval.

'Someone can pack for you,' her grandfather protested, throwing a look towards Karim.

Eva shook her head. 'I like to feel as if I actually have a

purpose in life,' she said, thinking, *Could I sound more self-pitying*?

She just made it to the door before the tears began.

The flight the next morning was an early one to fit in with her grandfather's schedule. Knowing King Hassan's dislike of tardiness, she was packed and ready and feeling mad with herself because she minded that Karim had made no attempt to say goodbye or even wish her a safe journey.

The Brownie points she had gained from being early were lost when, on the point of leaving, Eva realised she had left her toiletry bag upstairs.

Her grandfather clicked his tongue in irritation as she flew up the stairs two at a time.

Typically, given the urgency, she could see it nowhere; having ransacked her bedroom and bathroom she suddenly remembered the dressing room!

It was actually a small antechamber lined with mirrors that joined her suite of rooms to Karim's. It had not seen a lot of use recently, but she had gone in trying to see the back of her hair as she had attempted a swept-up style she had copied from a magazine that morning.

It had not made her look elegant; it had made her look about five!

Had she carried the bag in there with her?

She ran through the bathroom and into the corridor. She was inside before she realised that she was not alone.

Karim was standing there wearing nothing but a very small towel looped around his middle.

'I...I...' Losing the fight not to look, her eyes slid down his body. Things deep inside her tightened; he really was beautiful. A deep throb of longing slid through her. 'I left my... This... I'm late.'

He was looking at her in a way that made her heart race. He cleared his throat and ran a hand across his stubble-covered jaw.

Eva thought about the stubble grazing her skin and the tactile image was so strong she had to grab the radiator to steady herself.

'Have a safe journey.'

The anticlimax was intense. 'You too,' she heard herself babble stupidly. Then she improved on her impersonation of a total fool by clutching her head and groaning.

'Are you ill?'

His voice, rough with concern, was close by; she knew all she had to do was turn around and she could lay her head on his chest.

She fought off the mad impulse and shook her head. 'No, just…' Her eyes brushed his. 'Totally…totally… Goodbye.' Eyes on the ground, she brushed past him and grabbed the offending item and then, like a scared rabbit, she thought, wincing every time she mentally replayed the scene later, she scuttled away, her heart pounding like a piston.

It was actually good to meet up with her new and bewilderingly large family when she arrived in Azharim; fielding comments on her marriage was less enjoyable. It was a veritable minefield of potential embarrassment. Keeping up the pretence in front of her clearly curious relatives—who only stopped asking direct questions in deference to an edict by her grandfather—gave her a permanent headache.

After the first couple of days time began to drag heavily and, as crazy as it seemed, she missed Karim—if the combination of the achy feeling lodged behind her breastbone, feeling restless, distracted and unable to concentrate constituted missing?

You chose to come here, she reminded herself.

And he didn't try and stop you.

The necessary distraction came in the form of her neglected thesis. Instead of moping and soul-searching, Eva decided to put some serious work in on her almost-completed doctoral dissertation.

Never had she shown more enthusiasm for the boring detail of collating statistics, and, despite her initial scepticism on her ability to concentrate, the work did get done.

She was putting the finishing touches to her thesis, an occasion that only recently had been her total focus in life, when she received news that Karim and Amira had been allowed to fly home by the doctors.

The urgency to get the final draft printed and bound faded.

They hoped, so the message said, to see Eva very soon.

It was as impersonal as the rest of the communications she had received from Karim. While he had made contact regularly during the three weeks she had been here, there was nothing in the impersonal e-mails she had received that could not have been read by her grandfather.

But as she had asked herself— *What else do you expect, Eva?*

Her problem was she had lost the ability to separate expectations and fantasies.

He wasn't likely to confide a yearning to hear her voice. Or indulge in a lot of gushing stuff about not being able to stop thinking about her.

They had not exactly parted on the best of terms and the man had a lot of things, more important things, on his mind.

But then maybe the things they needed to discuss were better spoken of face to face.

She tried to view the opportunity to do just that with hope rather than fear…and managed excitement and exhilaration that tipped over without warning into open gibbering panic.

As Eva arranged to leave on the next flight, she was on the excitement stomach-clenching stage, until, that was, a casual remark by one of her cousins revealed that Karim and his daughter had already been home a week.

Talk about being brought to earth with a bump!

Eva struggled to hide the sharp stab of hurt as the news

drained away every last trace of her buoyant mood. She was too depressed to manage even gibbering panic.

It must have shown in her face because good-natured Ruhi added, 'I expect he wanted to give the little one time to settle in before producing a new stepmother… That's always tricky.'

'I expect you're right.' *And thank you, Ruhi*, she thought, *for giving me something else to worry about*. She'd given so much time to the wife issue she'd not paused to consider the equally precarious role of stepmother.

Given this occurrence, it was hardly surprising that she was rather subdued when she arrived at the palace to meet her step-daughter, trying hard as she did so *not* to think about Karim's formal cold reception at the airport. Like a new over-hyped blockbuster, it had been a major anticlimax.

Even the incredible atrium with the mosaic ceiling of lapis lazuli failed to awaken her enthusiasm—she just kept seeing his expression when he had walked out to meet her on the tarmac.

Karim had looked at her as though she were a stranger, or at least someone he wished were a total stranger rather than the wife he had to take home to meet his daughter. Someone he was saddled with for the rest of his life.

The little girl, though, didn't notice any atmosphere between the adults. She showed no sign of illness as she literally bounced with excitement when she saw Eva.

She immediately became entranced by the colour of Eva's hair and announced she wanted her own hair to be that colour when it grew back, just like her new mama.

Eva had a lump in her throat when she told her that she had always wanted black hair and people rarely liked what they had. The little girl was allowed to have tea with them before she was ushered away for a nap by her nurse.

With a spontaneous display of affection she climbed on Eva's knee and hugged her before her nurse dragged her away.

'She's lovely.' Eva had been conscious of Karim's silent presence, but while the child was there she had not been forced to actually look at him.

She did so now and she could do this. She wanted him, so why pretend? Even the scent of his skin from this distance was driving her totally crazy.

'Yes, she's a charmer.'

Obeying a compulsion he could not resist, his hooded glance slid over the soft contours of her face, greedily drinking in the details. Her skin was softer and even whiter than he remembered. The dimple in her cheek, though, was absent; she was not smiling.

She had not been smiling except for a faint tragic flicker when he had met her on the tarmac. The greeting had borne no resemblance to the one in his head, the one where she had flung herself into his arms.

It was ironic that what had displeased him would have pleased the small but vocal minority in the capital he had spent the last week identifying. After identifying them he had made a point of explaining that he would not look favourably on people who spread tales about his wife's past. They had been suitably chastened, but the situation would bear watching. It would be hard enough for Eva to adapt without the moral majority who thought a virgin bride was the only suitable mate for a future King talking behind their hands.

They could think what they liked, but he made no bones about how vigorous his response would be if he heard them.

Conscious that if he touched Eva his ability to pull back was in doubt, Karim had ignored the cheek she offered him. He had also ignored the discussion of the weather.

He had had more trouble ignoring her warm mention of Luke, who apparently had let her know that her tutor was extremely pleased with the final draft of her thesis.

If the man had been within his grasp he would have taken more than a little pleasure from spoiling his pretty face.

For a man who had always prided himself on his control it was shocking to suddenly have none, though not in the same shocking league as the almost audible sound of the floodgates that had held back his emotions for years buckling when he had seen her standing there on the tarmac.

Looking so small and lost and vulnerable, her hair like a beacon.

He had never wanted a woman in a way that defied logic and reason—he did now.

He had spent the previous three weeks since they had last been together—it would have been two if he hadn't arrived back and found more than a little bad feeling directed towards his new wife—alternating between feeling furious that he had allowed himself to be trapped for a second time into a marriage that was not convenient for him, and being furious with Eva for choosing to spend that time with her family and not with him and more specifically in his bed.

The fact he had made no attempt to stop her and had not disagreed with King Hassan's suggestion only increased the level of Karim's sense of impotent fury.

It was a lot of fury.

And at one level Karim was conscious that it was a lot easier to be angry than actually examine his feelings in any great depth. As they had driven in silence in the car with three feet and a wall of silence separating them he had repeated to himself like a mantra, This is just sex, this is just sex.

And when it was more than *imagined* sex he would be sane again.

Even repeating it twice did not make it sound true.

'And she's well.'

'Total remission,' he confirmed, dragging his thoughts from her mouth.

'That's marvellous,' Eva said, struggling to maintain a wary smile in the face of his grim forbidding expression. His body language was so rigid she could see the fine muscles just under the surface of the golden skin in his neck quivering.

Someone had to break the ice.

'I was wondering if perhaps we could…eat together tonight and…catch up?' Tonight she would come clean and admit her sexual inexperience was a lead weight around her neck.

She also planned to admit that sex with him and only him was not something she would have a problem with.

Karim, feeling the tension that he always felt preceding a visit to his father, a tension on this occasion made a hundred times worse by the fact he wanted her so badly he could taste it, shook his head.

He would have delayed the visit had the nurse in charge of the team who cared for his father not confided her concerns about the King's health. Just what did *deterioration* mean?

'I'm afraid that I have plans. I'll be away until Friday,' he said, struggling to make small talk because he was seeing her naked and underneath him…and on top of him.

Eva swallowed and smiled through the rejection, determined he would never guess how much he had hurt her. The message could not have been clearer. First he had bundled her off to her grandfather, been back home a week before he bothered suggesting she join them, and now she had arrived he couldn't wait to leave.

Well, this time she was taking the hint!

'Would you like to see this garden? Amira has this idea that she—'

He was pretending to be polite. He had clearly spent the last three weeks wishing this marriage had never happened, comparing it no doubt with his first marriage, and Eva couldn't bear it another second.

Her voice cold and crisp, she cut across him. 'No…that is, actually I'm pretty tired. I could do with a nap…if you'll excuse me.' *Let it never be said I don't have lovely manners*, she thought as she walked straight-backed from the room.

And lovely posture, and who, she asked herself, needs sex when they have posture? At least she could look royal even if she didn't feel royal inside.

CHAPTER NINE

KARIM hadn't been away the three days he had said, but an entire week.

He had got back the day before the reception to introduce Eva to the great and good was scheduled. An event that had taken on awesome and daunting significance in her mind.

Now, about to accompany him to the reception, she said, 'I can't do this.' And he was a selfish monster to imagine she could. Back and not a damned word about where he'd been or with whom!

Karim tore his eyes from her neckline and the creamy cleft between her breasts. 'You don't have to do anything. Just be charming.'

The instruction made her roll her eyes in angry despair that was not feigned. 'How?'

'If in doubt say nothing.' It was not as easy as it sounded. Saying nothing when he had wanted to say all he could think about was sinking into her, or saying nothing when he wanted to tell her he wanted to kiss her and have her taste him in her mouth had not been as easy as it sounded.

It had been hell!

He felt simultaneously torn and guilty—torn between his duty to his father and his desire to be with his new wife, and guilt that the duty weighed so heavily.

He had arrived to discover that his father's condition had

indeed deteriorated, to a degree that was painful to observe. To see the once robust man a broken and frail shadow of his former self had made him want to turn and run like a coward, but of course he had not followed his shameful base instincts—he had kissed his father and soothed him when he flinched.

It had taken time but after a week, and with several changes in his drug regime, he had left his father as well as he would ever be.

Now he was back and all the talk was of this damned reception. *Dieu*, he could not understand why he had arranged it. To make Eva's transition easier by introducing her to his world had been his idea… Right now the last thing he felt like doing was sharing her. The hunger in his body roared like a furnace.

'That should make a great impression—a dumb wife.'

It amazed her that as an intelligent man it hadn't occurred to him that a simple confidence-boosting lie—*You look incredible*—would have worked fine and might have given her the courage and confidence she needed.

A kiss might have helped, but that wasn't going to happen unless she asked… It had to be her choice, a choice made all the more difficult by the obvious fact—it was hard to interpret his disappearing act any other way—Karim intended to carry on with his life just as he had before he had married.

She had to face facts and not carry on clinging to a fantasy.

When she had asked Tariq outright where Karim was, to say the man had been cagey was an understatement. He had dripped guilt.

His response that *he wasn't sure* would not have fooled a baby—Tariq always knew where Karim was. He was generally one step behind, so Karim wanted his privacy—to Eva's way of thinking there was only one possible reason for his strange behaviour: Karim had been with a mistress.

It all fitted.

And yet last night she had gone to his room…what was wrong with her? Her cheeks burned with mortified heat at the memory. Of course it had been with the intention of laying down some rules of her own—*her story and she was sticking to it.*

He'd asked her to think about what she wanted and she had and she wanted an exclusive relationship or no relationship at all. Fighting talk, but who knew what she would have accepted? She had a tendency to forget she had any pride when it came to Karim, she thought miserably. He had entered her blood like a virus and she was consumed by the fever.

Well, she'd never know because she had gone to his room only to find his bed empty and untouched. She had returned to her own bed and lain there wondering where and, more importantly, *with whom* he had slept that night. It didn't seem likely that a virile and highly sexed man like Karim spent any night alone.

She had predictably cried herself to sleep, hence the puffy-eyed look today.

'A dumb wife—that really would make me the envy of every man present.' Karim knew he would already have the envy of every man present because they imagined that he was sharing a bed with his wife.

Not doing so was driving him slowly out of his mind.

Looking at him, tall and commanding, in his formal traditional clothes looking like the quintessence of virile masculinity, Eva knew she would be the envy of every woman present and also the focus of mass speculation.

There would be a lot more speculation if they knew that her husband didn't share her bed.

Eva cringed inwardly at the idea of anyone discovering her secret.

'Funny man,' she drawled. 'Do you have to work at being a total sexist?'

The question drew no reply.

As she walked with him towards the ballroom where the reception was being held she felt her resentment rise. No wonder she had no confidence—not only did her husband not want to sleep with her, but he kept mistresses, possibly an entire harem! When she had walked into his study in her finery he had looked her up and down, and made no comment.

She had interpreted his silence as disappointment, which was a blow because frankly this was as good as it got!

Eva told herself that it wasn't that she needed his approval, just a little support when she was facing the daunting prospect of being judged by, if not the entire world, his world.

'Ready?'

Glancing in the full-length mirror behind Karim, she saw a total stranger standing there.

A stranger with upswept hair. She touched the stunning emeralds that Karim had casually presented to her as if they were no big deal to wear around her neck.

Panic growing in the pit of her belly, she started to shake her head... 'No, I'm not ready. I can't do this...I...'

Karim knew she was speaking, he could see her lips, but he could not hear for the roaring of the pressure inside his head.

A pressure that had been building for the past weeks, but when she had appeared wearing that dress and he had wanted to do nothing but peel it off it had cranked up several painful notches.

He had been shaking so hard that he was amazed she didn't appeared to notice; he had not trusted himself to speak. His control had teetered on a knife's edge.

Now as he looked down into her beautiful face he knew that tonight he was going to spend the night in her bed; last night he had held back from going to her only because she had looked at him with such obvious resentment when he had offered no explanation for his absence.

He had wanted to, but a lifetime's habit was hard to break and he didn't know how to share his grief, but he did know that if he had gone to her last night the story of his week with his father would have come out.

Eva would have seen his pain… A man should be able to deal with what life threw at him. Karim had always viewed sharing private feelings and emotions as a weakness—would Eva see it as a weakness?

For the first time in his life he found himself caring about what a woman thought of him.

He pushed away the thought and slid his hands to her shoulders. He could see her lips stop moving. He carried on staring at the soft lush outline as in his mind he tugged down the bodice off her shoulders to reveal her perfect breasts.

He imagined the texture of her skin, the taste of it. He imagined moving inside her, hearing her cry his name.

Then imagination was not enough to silence the roaring in his head. He had not known a moment's peace since they met and knew he wouldn't until he possessed her. She was like a fever in his blood.

His chest lifted and with a groan he bent his head to hers.

He put all the weeks of longing and frustration into the kiss, bending her supple spine back over his arm with the pressure of it, causing the pins in her hair to loosen. He tangled his fingers in the silky curtain that spilled down her back and pulled her face to his as he kissed her with an almost frenzied desperation.

He felt the vibration of her throaty moan as he slid his hands over the curves of her slim body. She leaned bonelessly into him as he nipped and licked at her lush parted lips, tasting, sliding inside her mouth and meeting her tongue with his own.

Finally coming up for air, he lifted his head.

They stared at one another in stunned silence, a silence that was finally broken by Eva's inarticulate whisper of, 'My God! You…'

Eva sucked in a sighed breath and pressed a hand to her trembling lips. At night when she had lain awake wanting him she had told herself the kiss had not been that fantastic, it had just been the overheated emotions of the day that had built it up into something exceptional in her mind.

'Eva—'

'You really are very *very* good at that.'

His eyes darkened.

It was Tariq at his shoulder, tactfully clearing his throat, that made Karim recall his surroundings.

'Your absence has been noted.'

'Yes, we will be there directly.' He looked down at Eva. 'You are ready now?'

She nodded. She was ready to do anything he wanted.

Her pliant state of shock lasted long enough for Karim to steer her in front of him into the glittering hall and the hundreds of waiting finery-clad people.

He'd definitely distracted her from her panic attack...that couldn't be why he had kissed her, could it?

No, she told herself, he wouldn't be that calculating, but once the seeds of doubt were planted they were hard to ignore.

The alternative explanation was impulsive lust or his feelings getting the better of him, but, as she knew only too well, he'd had no trouble controlling his lust up until now.

Did it matter? He'd kissed her and with any luck he'd do it again.

Karim, who was standing a little distance away, performing the hand-shaking, cheek-kissing, head-bowing ritual that Eva was, watched from the corner of his eyes until he was satisfied she was coping.

'She'll need your support tonight.'

Karim turned his head to acknowledge King Hassan. 'She has my support, but you underestimate her. Eva can do more than she thinks. All she lacks is confidence.'

A little later, having watched his cousin monopolise her for ten minutes, Karim chose a lull to excuse himself and move to her side.

'Are you all right?'

She shivered as his breath brushed her cheek. 'I'm not sure yet,' she admitted, his kiss still dominating her thoughts.

'Me too.' Before she could question the oddly cryptic remark her grandfather appeared at her side and Eva was obliged to give him her attention.

Her grandfather was not the only head of state present. There were a number of influential foreign guests, but most of his countrymen, like Karim, were dressed traditionally, and while many of the women's clothes had a distinct Eastern influence most had a Western twist. About half of them wore their heads uncovered, though this did not make Eva feel any less conspicuous as she was the only redhead present.

This was not her sort of thing, though the mingling and smiling graciously was proving a lot easier than she had imagined.

Eva's smile slipped when she was formally introduced to the possible reason for Karim's absence from his bed.

The moment Eva saw Layla Al Ahmed she heard alarm bells, which she dismissed as paranoia, but when she saw the beautiful brunette look at Karim through her heavily made-up almond-shaped eyes things fell horribly into place.

Feeling sick to her stomach, she injected a few more volts into her forced smile as the thickset man with Layla stepped forward to present himself while the curvaceous brunette chatted animatedly to Karim.

'Layla has a successful career in interior design,' explained her proud father, who was, it transpired, one of Karim's economic advisors, as well as the head of one of the country's oldest and most powerful families.

Her credentials, as well as her curves, were impeccable.

'My daughter is very talented. She could have done anything.'

And if her great career failed she could make a fortune in advertising uplift bras—not that the gorgeous brunette needed one, Eva thought, hitching her bodice a little higher on her more modest cleavage and gathering the light embroidered silk stole she wore over it a little tighter.

'She and Karim were virtually brought up together,' he confided as they watched Karim kiss first one of her bejewelled hands and then her cheeks.

'And some people,' he continued, 'thought that after Karim overcame his bereavement they might...' He shrugged and smiled. 'But Karim is a rule unto himself, as I am sure you know.'

He bowed and moved away, leaving Eva to wonder if he had intended to plant the idea that the pair had been virtually engaged in her head and was it true?

Had Layla been the reason that three days had turned into seven? Had he been unable to tear himself away from her side? Would Karim have married the lovely and very suitable Layla if things had not happened as they did?

Stomach churning, she pushed the question away and responded to the French Ambassador's wife who had introduced herself as Julia and was admiring the emeralds and comparing them to Eva's eyes.

When Karim appeared at her shoulder she greeted him like an old friend and repeated the compliment, adding, 'Your wife's French is quite, quite excellent and isn't she coping well? I remember the first Embassy Ball I hosted—my smile had to be surgically removed.'

Eva felt warmed by the compliment, but the glow of pleasure faded abruptly when, after acknowledging that her French was *adequate*, Karim added, 'Let's hope she doesn't take too long to master Arabic, Julia.'

Eva's chin went up. 'I hope so too. Then people will have to be out of earshot when they talk about me.' She could not shake the conviction that the lovely Layla's laughter had been aimed at her or the image of her in bed with Karim.

Karim arched a brow and said, 'Paranoia, Eva?' And left her standing there feeling like a total idiot.

Julia took her arm and patted her hand. 'Layla is what I'd call a man's woman…'

Eva shot her a startled glance. Were her thoughts that transparent?

'Men look,' Julia continued with a Gallic shrug. 'It is in their nature.' Her grin deepened and she added with mock sympathy, 'Poor lambs. You know, when I married Alain I went through agonies thinking he lusted after every woman he smiled at. Alain could have anyone he chose, you see, then one day it finally struck me—he chose me.'

Eva bit back the impulse to assure the Frenchwoman that as far as she was concerned Karim could smile at any woman he pleased, but she could hardly reveal to her sympathetic and obviously romantic friend that she was no more in love with her husband than he was with her.

'It's a steep learning curve,' she admitted. The Frenchwoman had no idea how steep!

She wondered what her new friend's reaction would be if she explained that Karim had only married her because honour had demanded it and it wasn't politically expedient for him to alienate his influential neighbour.

Of course, as far as she was concerned Karim could romance whom he liked, but he might at least have the decency and good manners not to rub her nose in it!

Eva's resentment and sense of isolation increased when Karim, presumably having adopted a sink-or-swim policy, left her to her own devices for the next half-hour.

It was not relief she felt when she caught sight of her tall, supremely elegant husband returning. Her heart rate began to thud with a confusing mixture of excitement, resentment and apprehension.

He reached her side and bent forward, bringing his face close to hers; for a moment she thought he was going to kiss her again.

He didn't.

'Smile, and stop looking at me as if I'm the wolf and you're Little Red Riding Hood.' His hooded glance slid to the hint of creamy cleavage pressing against the pale satin and he wondered if her skin tasted as good as it looked.

It would not be so very difficult to eat her up. 'You're meant to be enjoying yourself.'

Shaking a little from the anticlimax, she fixed him with a narrow-eyed glare. 'Well, I'm not—not enjoying myself.'

'You seemed to be enjoying yourself when you were talking to my cousin.'

'Cousin? Could you be a bit more specific? You do have hundreds.'

'Hakim.'

'Oh, the doctor—yes, he's really nice.'

'That's what all the girls think before he breaks their hearts.'

She watched him walk away with a puzzled frown. Anyone who didn't know the circumstances might have confused his attitude with jealousy. Next time she saw him the orchestra had struck up a slow number that drew several couples to the floor.

Eva, uncertain of the protocol, turned to him for clarification and found he was watching her with an expression that she struggled to decipher. 'Are we meant to dance?'

Karim, already in a state of arousal, was skeptical of his ability even in his loose robes to hold her in his arms and not reveal the fact to everyone present.

'I don't dance,' he said, but he did other things well and tonight he planned to show her.

That had been ten minutes earlier and she could still see his face when he said it, still hear his dismissive tone.

She was hearing it as she listened to what Julia's extremely handsome and charming husband was saying. Eva's own smile had become fixed and strained—she hoped in an intelligent way, but the fact was she was finding it virtually impossible to concentrate on what her companion was saying.

Rage and a strong sense of misuse made her chest tight. She

struggled against a suffocating sensation to get her breath…was he trying to humiliate her?

Don't let anyone see you care. Don't let him see you care. Her lips compressed as her glance was once again drawn to the dance floor. She looked quickly away, a smile frozen on her face, thinking, *Don't let anyone see you care.*

Don't let him see you care!

Why did she care?

Presumably Karim's non-dancing stance only applied to dancing with her, because for someone who didn't dance he was managing rather well as he circled the floor with the high-born beauty in his arms.

They moved as one, bodies close, dark heads closer, the diamonds around Layla's wrists and lovely neck catching the lights of the chandeliers overhead.

Eva had struggled hard against the irrational dislike she had felt earlier when the brunette had been introduced, but she now stopped trying—call it a personality clash.

Call it jealousy, said the voice in her head.

Logically she had no reason to dislike a woman she had not exchanged more than a dozen words with, if you discounted the way she touched Karim at every opportunity and spoke to him in that husky voice pitched too low for anyone else to hear, but obviously what she said was witty because Karim laughed more than once, looking younger and more relaxed as he did so than Eva had ever seen him.

The music stopped and Eva expelled a relieved sigh that drew an amused look from the man beside her. She said something to cover the moment, aware in the periphery of her vision of Karim bowing his head to his dance partner, but before he could leave Layla took his hand, tilting her head and pouting as she moved in close and whispered something in his ear.

Eva gave up all pretence of making conversation and watched, her eyes as hard as the emeralds around her neck as Karim shook his head, trying—not very hard, it seemed to

Eva—to leave before he allowed his partner to drag him back to the centre of the dance floor. She could hear from where she was standing the tinkling sound of the brunette's laughter as she laid her fingers against Karim's neck.

Eva watched them dance, but she wasn't the only one who did so. She knew that several glances were cast in her direction and the voltage of her smile and the level of her animation rose in direct proportion to the interest.

Finally when she laughed too loudly at something, Alain leaned forward with an expression of genuine concern and asked softly, 'Are you all right?'

It was at that moment it hit her.

She shook her head slowly, a stunned look on her face as her glance slid towards the dance floor where Karim was moving, his grace and co-ordination matched by those of his partner.

'No, I'm not all right.' *I'm in love with my husband.*

Now how stupid was that?

She shook her head. It wasn't possible!

She obviously had spoken the latter aloud because though Alain was looking at her with concern it was not the sort of alarm someone would reserve for a bride who was having a breakdown at the possibility she was in love with her husband.

'Shall I get someone…Karim…?'

The suggestion made her eyes widen with horror. 'No, not Karim!'

Her vehemence appeared to take the Frenchman aback, but he smiled and said tentatively, 'A glass of water?'

'That would be nice,' she said, thinking, *Pull yourself together, Eva, at least until you get out of here.* 'There's no need to worry Karim,' she added.

Alain nodded, but did not look entirely convinced by her addition and, catching sight of herself in the reflective surface of a plate-glass window, Eva was not surprised. The only colour in her face was the green of her eyes, which looked enormous in her pale face.

She pressed her fingers to her temples where the thudding intensified as the pressure in her head increased.

Getting out of here was her one coherent thought in a brain that was seething with confusing and ambiguous thoughts. As soon as the Frenchman moved out of view she made her way towards the open glass doors.

People had spilled out into the enclosed courtyard where the sound of tinkling fountains was a pleasant background noise to conversation.

Her heels clicked on the mosaic floor as she exchanged a few comments with people. She had no idea what she said, but presumably she must have made sense, unless they were just politely ignoring the fact that she was talking gibberish.

As she stepped through a large metal-banded door and into the corridor beyond, closing the door behind her, the almost monastic silence hit her.

CHAPTER TEN

CLOSING HER EYES AS she pressed her shoulders into the wall, Eva felt the tears begin to seep from under her lashes.

Angrily she brushed them away and straightened up.

She sniffed and inhaled. 'Don't get hysterical, Eva. This isn't love…it's sexual attraction and it will pass.' She began to laugh as the irony struck her that she was upset because there was a possibility she was in love with her own husband.

'Now how crazy is that?' she asked the painting that showed a stern man with a nose like Karim's looking noble astride a flashing-eyed stallion.

He didn't comment, neither did any of the servants she encountered as she walked through a maze of corridors with no particular idea of where she was going. Being the boss's wife had some perks and there was no sign of her shadows.

When some time later she found herself outside and near a gated entrance to the compound, the idea of escaping, at least temporarily, was too strong to resist.

Maybe outside without people watching her every move she'd be able to think straight? She held her breath as she walked past the armed guards and expelled it again when they made no attempt to detain her as she left the palace compound that was situated a few miles outside the capital, whose lights illuminated the horizon to the south.

When she had last passed along this well-lit palm-lined

avenue it had been seething with people; now it was totally deserted. Recalling Karim's rather stern lectures on security and the dangers of the desert, she felt a faint twinge of anxiety but she pushed it away.

This was not the desert, it was a street with electric lights. She could have been anywhere except there was no litter, and there were no sprawling suburbs—civilisation stopped abruptly and gave way to desert. Karim himself had told her that there was virtually no crime here.

She was perfectly safe and she was allowed to take a walk if she felt like it. She lifted her chin to a defiant angle. Karim probably wouldn't even notice she wasn't there.

And if she was needed Eva had no doubt Layla would be only too happy to deputise.

You're not in prison, Eva, she told herself.

But she was—a beautiful luxurious prison, but nonetheless that was what it was and what made it worse was she had walked inside, locked the door, thrown away the key and fallen for her jailer!

She shook her head and muttered, 'No, it's just sex.'

Her brooding thoughts returned to the reception. Was it just sex with Layla or was Karim in love with the curvaceous brunette?

Perhaps that was why a sexless marriage did not seem to bother him in the slightest—he had the lissom Layla to keep him warm when the sun went down.

The graphic images that went with this line of speculation made Eva's stomach churn sickly. Her hands balled into fists as she barred her teeth in a determined grimace; she was going to get the truth out of him if it killed her!

She had been here long enough to know how palace gossip worked and she was sure that if Layla was his mistress she was probably the only person who didn't know! The humiliation of being an object of pity was something she just could not bear.

She couldn't bear their unconsummated marriage, and the

irony was that her celibacy had never bothered her before. She had occasionally speculated on what she was missing—now what she was missing was driving her slowly insane.

The trouble was it wasn't exactly a level playing field. He was the world's sexiest man and not exactly inexperienced, while her experience consisted of a couple of goodnight kisses and a narrow escape from a supposed friend who had turned into a groper when they'd shared a taxi.

How did you confess to a man who thought you were some sort of sexual expert that you were in fact clueless?

A clueless virgin!

Did he know she couldn't think of anything else but him?

Of course he knew… With a grimace of self-disgust she shook her head angrily. You could only take self-deception so far…and Karim *not* knowing that her bones ached with longing when he was near was about as likely as him not touching her because he was afraid of rejection!

And now there was the further complication of Layla, who was not clueless or flat-chested and had possibly spent the last week in his bed.

An emotional rush of misery rushed up to clog Eva's throat and with a sniff she hitched her narrow skirt that was making it hard to walk above her knees and tucked a long strand of hair that had been pulled free of her elegant topknot behind her ear.

The strong warm wind that blew in from the desert immediately swept it back into her eyes.

With a disconsolate sigh she left it there and thought… Are they having an affair?

The possibility brought a militant light to her eyes; if he thought she was going to put up with him installing Layla as his official mistress, he could think again! Eva's pace quickened in response to the energising rush of anger that swept through her body.

Karim should have told her about Layla; she had a right to know before she committed herself. Though as *not* committing herself would have made her responsible for destabilising an entire region and destroying economic progress it was extremely doubtful that her decision would have been different.

This was not what she had signed up for.

She had been so lost in her dark reflections that Eva had walked on several hundred yards before she realised she had run out of streetlamps.

With a sigh she turned and began to reluctantly retrace her footsteps, slowly now as the anger that had consumed her had burnt itself out.

As she walked she became aware that the buffeting wind had increased in strength and while it should be on her back now it was actually everywhere, hitting her from all sides.

She bent her head as the sand in the air stung her face.

She had not gone a few feet before she became aware that she was in trouble: the lights above were barely visible through the sand that stung and bit into every exposed inch of her skin. She couldn't see where the road surface ended and the desert began and the tall turrets and gleaming spires of the royal palace were barely visible.

Mind-numbing panic running just beneath the surface of her paper-thin stoic calm, she refused to recognise it as she told herself that it was lucky she had not strayed from the highway or walked far.

All she had to do was walk in a straight line.

'How difficult can that be?'

A few minutes later she was forced to acknowledge that her forced jovial comment had been a classic case of tempting fate. The surface she now stumbled over was not tarmac, it was uneven and rocky. Even if she had been able to lift her head there was no point—the visibility was nil, the world was black and the sand cut into every exposed inch of tender flesh without mercy.

She coughed, unable to breathe as she dropped to her knees

and wrapped her arms around herself in a futile attempt to protect her face.

There was nothing in her world but the noise of the storm, a roar all around…inside her head, everywhere. A strange sense of calm descended over her as she huddled there. Someone who was going to die ought not to feel so calm.

Eva began to lift her head…the expected sting on her face was not as bad as she had anticipated. Had the storm abated slightly? A tiny grain of hope took root and somewhere deep inside the instinct for survival stirred.

'I can't die! I don't want to die!'

If she died Karim would marry Layla.

'That's not my plan, either.'

When he had first spotted what looked like a bundle of rags Karim had thought the worst, then as the bundle had moved and he'd heard her speak a surge of relief had flooded his body.

His relief was tempered by the realisation that if he had chosen another path he would never have found her. He might have passed within yards of her…

He was not normally a person who dwelt on what *might* have been, but he struggled not to dwell on the narrowly diverted disaster as he reminded himself that they were not home and dry yet.

Hearing things could not be a good sign; Eva lifted her head and forced her reluctant eyelids to part. The voice was not in her head, it was in her ear.

The storm had not abated; it was a man's body and more precisely his chest, broad and incredibly comforting, that sheltered her from the extremes of the sandstorm.

Karim had found her.

'Karim? You shouldn't have come—now you'll die too!' she wailed.

The wind tugging and dragging at his white robes, he knelt before her, appearing immune as the rocks to the wind and sand.

His eyes above the cloth that covered his lower face blazed like the stars that had been blotted by the sandstorm.

He bent his head close to hers like a lover, but there was nothing loverlike in the words he yelled in her ear. 'Nobody is going to die. If the storm kills you it will deny me the pleasure of throttling you with my own hands!'

'I—'

'Shut up!'

Before Eva could respond to this autocratic decree she found herself drawn against his body. She gasped and stiffened, then sighed as a hand behind her head forced her face into his shoulder.

Karim, holding her, found himself caught between rage and tenderness.

Eva tried to lift her head but he pushed it back down. 'What are you doing?'

'I'm thinking.'

He was also stroking her hair in the middle of the raging storm; the small act of tenderness brought tears to her eyes. Eva closed her eyes, feeling his body heat and his strength slowly seep into her bones; for the first time she allowed herself to think that she stood a realistic chance of surviving this.

She was vaguely conscious of the sound of ripping cloth, but did not connect it with her own designer gown. Then as he rose she felt herself enfolded, not just by his arms, but by the flowing fabric of his robe, which he had wrapped around her. He placed a hand under her behind and without waiting to be instructed Eva automatically wrapped her legs around his middle, a voice in her head that clearly did not appreciate the seriousness of the situation saying she could get used to this.

'Hold on!'

The instruction was unnecessary—she already was!

Having found it impossible to stay upright herself, Eva couldn't believe that Karim could move forward with the additional burden of her weight. Above the sound of the storm that raged around them, with her head pressed into his shoulder, Eva was conscious of the heavy thud of his heartbeat.

She held tight, closed her ears, concentrated on the sound, felt the moisture leak from under her eyelids and as love for him filled her it was a relief to finally stop fighting the realisation.

What if she never had a chance to tell him how she felt? She felt the salty moisture leak from her eyes.

'Not far now,' Karim shouted in her ear. Fuelled by the adrenaline rushing through his veins and acting on nine parts instinct and one part sheer desperation, he hoped that he was telling the truth.

Eva wanted to ask, Not far from where? But she didn't have the strength; it was all she could do to hang onto him. Her arms and legs were trembling with the effort of holding on.

How did he keep going? she wondered as Karim continued to make steady progress, not moving swiftly but with assurance; once or twice she could sense him testing his footing before he continued.

The almost animal screech of the whipping wind and whirling sand had filled her head and hurt her senses for so long that when it stopped abruptly it was disorientating.

She opened her eyes and there was nothing but inky, impenetrable blackness. She could still hear the keening cry of the wind but it was a background noise.

We're safe…we're safe, she thought, too relieved to wonder where they were or how he had found their sanctuary.

'Wait here.'

Wait where? she thought.

Placed on her feet and without the supporting strength of his strong arms, Eva sank to the ground. It felt cold and hard against her bare legs.

'Don't leave me!' she begged, not giving a damn about pride as she clung onto his leg in the pitch darkness.

The anger Karim had been forced to hold in check was once

more frustrated, now by the note of pure panic in her tremulous voice. The vulnerability she so often struggled to hide behind a tough exterior was right there and it awakened protective instincts he hadn't known he possessed.

She nearly died... He pushed away the thought because he knew if he let it take hold he would not be able to control the rage that continued to simmer just below the surface. He would finish rescuing her and then he would throttle her, he promised himself.

He unfurled her fingers and retained them in his hand as he dropped to his knees beside her. Reaching out, he found her face and framed it with his free hand, rubbing the dust from the curve of her cheek as he did so.

'You will stay here. I will find some light, all right?'

There was a pause before she nodded, wondering where on earth he was going to find light. She shivered when his fingers fell away, the loss of physical contact making her feel utterly bereft, and she knew there was a lot more to her reaction than a simple fear of dark strange places. She craved his touch with an intensity that was just as primal as the survival instinct that had made her fight the storm.

'I won't go far,' he promised.

He didn't. Eva could hear him as she sat in the darkness, her teeth chattering more with reaction than cold, listening to the sounds of him moving around. He swore once when he obviously collided with something, then there was a scratching and scuffing sound, then light.

It came from an old-fashioned kerosene lamp that Karim held aloft.

Eva blinked as her eyes adjusted slowly.

Looking around, she was able to distinguish a crude table set against one wall. A chair stood beside it, another lay overturned. There were several assorted items that suggested this place had once been occupied.

'Where is this place?' Eva asked, rubbing her hand along the smooth stone surface she sat on. The walls around and above them had the same pale sand appearance. '*What* is it?'

Holding the light, Karim moved closer and, brushing some debris off the crude table, placed it down on the scratched surface.

'Just like home,' she joked shakily. 'Though with slightly less gold leaf.'

Karim felt his admiration grow as he watched her produce a shaky smile.

How many women who had been through what she had would joke? Most he could think of would right now be having hysterics, hysterics that would have filled him with impatience. She was smiling—shaking like a leaf but smiling—and he was filled with... A flicker of shock registered in his eyes as he recognised the emotion that made him want to gather her in his arms as tenderness.

It seemed it was possible to want to throttle a woman and protect her from the slightest breeze at one and the same time; possible, but not comfortable.

He had not been comfortable since he met his Princess.

Eva's wandering gaze found his face and lingered, the breath snagging painfully in her throat. The gold-tinged glow radiated by the flickering light cast shadows over Karim's face, highlighting the strength and purity of his fabulous bone structure.

He was beautiful!

So beautiful it hurt; it hurt physically.

Her lashes swept protectively downwards as things deep inside her clenched and tightened. She was filled with deep, hopeless yearning. If these feelings she could not articulate never went away, how would she bear it?

'There are a series of caves in the rock face. Up until ten years ago some were still occupied, but once there was an entire community living here.'

'Nobody lives here now?' She tried to ignore the strange heaviness in the air that had little to do with the storm that raged outside and instead imagined the silent place filled with the buzz of people going about their lives, living and loving… It was difficult to visualise.

'You're not seeing it at its best,' he observed, stamping his boots without taking his eyes from her face.

An edge in his deep voice made her look up at him. The light was not strong enough for her to read his expression, but Eva found the fixed intensity of his stare unnerving.

She looked away and, aware of her heart pounding against her breastbone, drew a line with her finger in the fine layer of sand that covered the stone floor.

She forced an awkward smile. 'You're not seeing me at my best, either.'

CHAPTER ELEVEN

BUT he was seeing her—you'd think he never had before, the way he was staring, his heavy-lidded regard still trained unblinkingly on Eva's face as he pulled off his head-covering and dragged a hand through his dark hair.

'You look exhausted!' he observed, feeling a stab of self-recrimination. The dust did not disguise the dark smudges of fatigue beneath her eyes.

As Eva's gaze swept protectively downwards her attention was captured by a painted item lying in the dust. A frown of enquiry forming between her brows, she picked it up.

Karim watched her brush the dust off the broken toy very carefully, his eyes widening with shock as he caught himself wondering if he would choose to end this marriage given the choice?

The speculation was pointless—it was not his choice to make.

'It's a doll.' When her gaze lifted to his her luminous eyes shone with unshed tears. 'I wonder what happened to the girl who owned it…did she cry when she lost it?' For some reason the idea of the lost doll and the lost community struck an emotional chord with Eva.

His lips curled into a cynical smile. 'People discard things when they are broken and sometimes when they are not,' he observed drily, thinking about his late wife's reaction to the birth of her daughter. She had made clear she hadn't wanted *a girl*.

Eva's fingers tightened around the carved wooden toy as she leapt on his comment. 'Are you saying *we* are broken?' Broken implied they had ever been intact—a whole, but their fake marriage was a sham. She gave a grimace of distaste as her eyes slid to the rings that adorned her left hand. 'You want an annulment?' The idea should make her feel relieved. This was what she wanted—a way to escape.

His spine stiffened. 'An annulment?'

Eva could feel the tension he radiated; the air around them vibrated with it. She gave a shrug. 'Why not?' Especially when there was someone so suitable just waiting to fill the vacancy.

His eyes narrowed. 'Is that what this stunt was about? You think if you act badly enough I will let you go?'

She winced at his choice of words. It made her feel like a bird in a cage—a luxurious solid gold-cage, but still a cage. She shook her head in revolted rejection of the idea and told him indignantly, 'It wasn't a stunt! Do you think I planned a sandstorm?' She gritted her teeth and cried, 'I'm trying my best to be what you want me to be…' Her energising burst of indignation vanished, leaving her feeling just incredibly weary.

She lifted her hands in a gesture of defeat. 'I'm just not very good at it.' That, she decided, tugging irritably at the torn bodice of her dress, was about the understatement of the century!

Karim swallowed. Her disconsolate little sigh tugged at his conscience and the exposed upper slopes of her breasts heightened the sexual frustration that he was fighting to control.

'I only want you to be yourself, Eva.'

She gave a disbelieving snort. 'What you want, Karim, is for me to vanish.' She lifted her chin in denial of the pain searing through her.

'What I want…' His jaw clenched as, despite exerting all his considerable mental control, he failed to banish the erotic image in his head of her small slim hands sliding down his body…her parted lips moving over… He inhaled sharply through flared nostrils and snarled, 'Don't be ridiculous!' It was not bad advice for a man who could not stop thinking about making love to his own wife.

A man who had furthermore said he wouldn't come to her bed until she asked for it. A night did not pass—a night, he was discovering, could be very long—when he did not regret the suggestion.

Eva couldn't read his silence any more than she could read his silver stare, but even without translation it was shredding her nerves.

Maybe, she mused, he was choosing his words carefully, but she had no doubt about what he would say if he articulated his displeasure. Duty was the tenet that Karim lived his life by, and she had failed in hers.

She had probably caused him and her family untold political and personal embarrassment. She could have attempted to defend her actions, but what would be the point? What was she meant to say—I went for a walk because I was sick with jealousy watching you dance with your mistress?

Just get it over with, she thought. A rant about the diplomatic incident her walking out had no doubt caused was preferable to this—anything would be preferable to this!

Nibbling her lower lip as she hunched her shoulders, she wiped a weary hand across her face and hoped she wasn't projecting the insecurity she was feeling.

'Ugh!' She grimaced when she felt the sand caked on her skin. She glanced down and closed one eye—it still didn't look any better!

She was not recognisable as the woman who had dressed for her first formal event. Well, she hadn't felt like a princess then, and now she didn't look like one, either!

Her once pristine virginal white dress—the irony of that had not been lost on Eva—was no longer white, neither was it in one piece. It was ripped up to thigh level and rent in several places.

If her face and hair were in a similar condition to the embarrassingly large expanses of exposed flesh on her legs, she was a wreck.

Suddenly it struck her as intensely funny that minutes after she had escaped a near-death experience she was worrying about her appearance.

A giggle rose in her throat; a little escaped before she clamped her lips tight.

'What is so funny?'

Eva, her green eyes glittering with unshed tears, raised her eyes to him. 'I am,' she told him, her voice rising to a quivering wail as she added, 'I am also incredibly shallow.'

The need to take her in his arms was almost overwhelming. 'This is shock.' The abruptness of his tone made her flinch.

'I...' Her swimming eyes lifted to his and hers lip began to quiver.

'Control yourself, Eva, you are *not* going to have hysterics.'

Eva gave a gulp and stared at him. 'Control? Are you even human? We nearly died out there...' She closed her eyes and shuddered.

A muscle clenched in his lean cheek. 'You want me to get in touch with my feminine side and weep?'

The satirical interjection brought her eyes open with a snap. 'And for the record you telling me not to do something makes me want to go right out and do it. Even though I'm far too old to become a rebel.'

'Useful information, but at this moment I have no time to employ reverse psychology, so I would be obliged if you simply do as I tell you. Of course, if you *wish* to have hysterics?' he inserted sardonically. 'If they are part of your bid for freedom, like walking out into the middle of a sandstorm?'

Eva had opened her mouth to deliver a pithy retort, then

suddenly she had a flashback to the moment when she had really imagined that she was never going to see him again.

The moment passed, but the emotional thickening in her throat still ached as she shook her head back and forth in a negative motion. 'I really wasn't trying to escape…I just…just…'

'Sit!'

The terse command cut across her fumbling explanation.

He repeated his instruction, adding a please, and righted an overturned wooden chair from the floor. She watched warily as he set it beside the table.

'You will crease your dress sitting on the floor.'

She looked from the hand he held out to her to his face and a quiver of a smile touched her lips as she stretched her hand to his. The quiver faded as their fingertips brushed; the wave of heat that passed through her body drew a dry gasp of shock from her throat.

She sat there staring at his fingers, struggling against the tidal surge of lust and yearning that paralysed her.

'Come.'

She tilted her head and their glances meshed. The air felt thick with tension as Karim enfolded her small hand in his.

'You're shaking.'

She tried to smile. 'I'm fine, just a little…' *in love*. Actually she was overwhelmingly, desperately in love.

When she had dreamt of being in love Eva had imagined it would be an uplifting, life-affirming experience, not this crushing weight. 'I lost a shoe,' she said, sitting down.

'I will buy you another shoe.' He reached down and dabbed his thumb to the tear that slid down her grubby cheek.

The tenderness in his action made her eyes fill again. 'For God's sake, don't be nice to me!' she pleaded in a shaky whisper.

'You've been through a terrible experience.'

Eva sniffed and said, 'You never had any problem being mean to me before… Do you want me to cry?'

'No!' Female tears had never had any effect on him previously, but each individual tear he watched etch a grimy path down her dusty cheeks felt like a knife thrust. In a more moderate tone he added, 'I have no wish to see you cry.'

'Then change the subject. Did you ever see this place when people lived here?'

He nodded. 'They were actually quite comfortable—cool in the summer and warm in winter.'

Eva watched him, mesmerised by the vibrancy of his voice. It was one of those occasions that she knew would remain imprinted on her memory, even when she was an old lady she would be able to recall the sound of his voice, little details like the sand adhering to his eyelashes and crusting his ebony brows.

God, but she loved him.

'If you know where they are you can see them from our apartments. They are only yards from the palace boundary.'

'Yards! I was only yards away...' She leaned back on her heels and gave an incredulous smile.

Karim had been fighting a losing battle to contain his anger since they had arrived in their sanctuary, but the smile broke him.

'What is wrong with you?'

She stared at him, startled by the abrupt change in his manner.

'Do you not appreciate how close you were to dying?'

Eva felt a wave of shamed contrition. It wasn't just her that nearly died. No wonder he was mad—she hadn't even thanked him.

'I'm really very grateful and I'm sorry I ruined the reception. I know there were a lot of important people there and I can't have made the best impression...and I ruined the dress and I know it cost a fortune.' She lifted a hand to her ear and added, 'One of my shoes is gone and I've lost an earring too, which is probably an heirloom.'

He regarded her with incredulity and dragged a not quite steady hand through his dusty hair. 'You think I care about *earrings*?' He shook his head and gritted, 'Do you lie awake thinking of ways to make me lose my temper?'

Fists clenched, her eyes sparkling, she glared up at him. 'No, I lie awake thinking…' She stopped, her eyes drifting to his mouth before they slid from his face.

'Thinking of what?'

Still unable to look at him, she could hardly tell the subject of her wakeful thoughts that all she thought about day or night was him… 'What can I say? You're so pretty when you're mad.'

The fire died from his face as he arched a questioning brow.

'It was a stupid thing to do. I suppose my grandfather is imagining me lying dead somewhere.'

'No,' Karim lied, thinking that Hassan probably was beside himself by this point. 'He knows you would be safe with me. Why, Eva?'

She lifted her tear-stained face to his and sniffed. 'Why what?'

'Why did you leave?' He couldn't bring himself to ask if it was connected with the kiss. The thought his kiss made her run was something he could not contemplate; it was something that made every bad thing that life had ever thrown at him pale into significance.

Eva thought of lying, but in the end she didn't have the energy.

'Everyone was watching you dance with Layla and they were probably wondering why you didn't marry her.'

'Layla?' he echoed, looking at her blankly.

'I know ours isn't a marriage in the real sense, but you might at least be discreet. You were all over her like a rash and I suppose you spent the last week with her too.'

'You're jealous!' The discovery did not appear to displease him.

Eva gritted her teeth and regarded him with a contemptuous

scowl. 'I suppose you like the idea of women fighting over you. Well, sorry, but I don't give a damn who you sleep with, but it's quite a different thing to flaunt your mistress in front of me. Given the circumstances of our marriage I didn't expect you to be monogamous,' she said, trying to sound reasonable. 'How would you like it if I flaunted my lover that way?'

'I would not like it at all.'

Eva, very conscious of the fact he had not denied having a lover, failed to notice the iron note of warning in his quiet voice.

'Well, I wouldn't do that to you.'

'Are you planning to take a lover any time soon?' he enquired in a conversational tone that was in stark variance to the gleam in his eyes.

'That's not the point.'

The red mist dancing before his eyes made it a struggle for Karim to concentrate. 'It is very much the point, Princess,' he contradicted with a face like stone. 'There will be no lover.'

Eva brought her teeth together in an incredulous smile; his hypocrisy was staggering. 'So you're going to be celibate too, are you?' she enquired in a conversational tone.

He paused, an expression she couldn't quite decipher flickering across his lean face, before he responded. 'I find that celibacy doesn't suit me!'

This virtual admission he intended to take a mistress sent a wave of white-hot fury through Eva. 'Great, so you can start a harem but I have to take up knitting. That's what I love about you—you're such a modern man!'

His lips twitched. 'You like knitting?'

Her eyes narrowed as she glared up at him. 'I hate knitting— it gives me a headache.'

'I would imagine that a harem would give me a headache. I can only cope with one woman at a time. You know, I do not think that celibacy suits you, either, Princess,' he observed, studying her flushed face.

She rolled her eyes. 'Everything is about sex with you!' she yelled even as she acknowledged her own hypocrisy.

Karim arched a brow. 'Everything is about sex with me? Possibly because it is something I am not getting.'

'Sure you're not!' she snarled with a contemptuous sniff. 'Well, you should be less cranky and distracted now that Layla is back in town,' she observed sourly.

'Layla Al Ahmed is an old family—'

Eva cut across him. 'Were you going to marry her?'

'Who told you that?'

Eva shrugged. 'It seems to be the consensus of opinion.'

'Well, opinion is wrong. There was never any possibility of my marrying Layla.'

She searched his face and he returned her scrutiny calmly. 'Really?'

'Really.'

'But she is your mistress?'

'I have no mistress. I am married, Eva.'

She swallowed and found she believed him; the rush of relief was weakening. 'I thought you might have forgotten. I don't feel married.'

'And how might I make you feel married—?' He stopped mid-sentence and said in a voice that lacked any inflection, 'Do not move.'

She opened her mouth to ask why not when he lunged towards her and slapped her open-handed on the shoulder. Her eyes opened wide in startled indignation that faded when she saw what he had in his fingers.

Eva shuddered. 'Is it poisonous?' The scorpion was certainly ugly.

Not responding to her question, Karim held the squirming bug at arm's length and said, 'I'll get rid of this.'

In the adjoining cavern he heard the distant but unmistakable sound of running water. Disposing of the scorpion, he followed it to its source.

The appearance of the toxic creature on Eva's bare skin had made his heart stop, but if nothing else it had driven home the bad taste of making love to your wife for the first time on the cold floor of a dusty cavern teeming with poisonous animal life.

The first time should be romantic. Such things he knew were important to women. For his part the place was irrelevant, and each extra second of waiting took a year off his life—but he would wait. He wanted it to be perfect.

CHAPTER TWELVE

Eva, waiting eagerly for his return, gave a sigh of relief when she heard his footsteps.

'This is all I could find,' Karim said, placing the earthenware bowl he carried on the table.

Eva saw it was full of water.

'You might like to wash…?'

The idea was appealing; the sand had got everywhere. 'Where did you get the water?'

'The water supply was cut off when the last occupant vacated, but deeper in the cave system there is an underground spring—it never dries up.

'Perhaps you could use these?' he suggested, producing as if by magic a pile of cotton sheets. 'They are rough but clean,' he said, placing them beside the earthenware bowl. He left without a word, pulling the thin curtain across the doorway as he did so.

Eva dipped her hand into the basin. The water in the basin was ice cold, but not as cold as his remote manner. The tears she was struggling to hold back stung the backs of her eyelids.

I will not cry, she told herself as she pulled down what remained of her zip and stepped out of the shredded dress.

Unclipping the strapless bra she wore under it, she leaned over the basin and splashed the cold water over her face and neck. It took her breath away, but felt good.

She tore a section off one of the rough cotton sheets and, using it like a facecloth, dipped it in the water and began to wipe the sand from her skin.

The process was painstaking and not exactly comfortable, leaving her skin tingling and pink.

Karim paused. There was no door to knock on.

His intention to tell her the storm was abating fled his brain the moment he pushed aside the curtain and stepped inside.

She stood with her back to him, naked but for a pair of pants that clung to the firm curves of her rounded behind.

Nailed to the spot, he stared. Her body was more perfect than he had imagined—and he had imagined. The desire that he had spent weeks constantly battling flared up, hot and out of control.

He made no attempt to subdue it, but allowed his hungry gaze to roam over the soft gentle flare of her hips, the soft, round, peachy perfection of her bottom and the shapely length of her slim, elegant legs.

He thought about those legs wrapping around him, pulling him tight into her, and a low moan was wrenched from his throat.

The sound made Eva start and spin around. He saw the shock on her face as she stood there, a wet cloth pressed to her breasts, covering most but not all; one tight, pouting nipple, pink and glistening with water droplets, peeped out.

The pulse of lust that slammed through his body drove the breath out of Karim's lungs in one gasp.

Eva met his stare and hot colour rushed to her cheeks as her lips parted in a silent gasp. 'I...' She stopped, lifted her chin and, with her eyes holding his, allowed her hands to slowly fall to her sides.

For a long moment their eyes stayed locked. Mesmerised by the burning heat in his bold, hungry stare, Eva felt her knees buckle and grabbed the table for support.

Karim's eyes dropped. He heard the groan but did not connect it with himself. The tight pink buds on her small but perfect breasts reacted to the brush of his eyes.

Eva saw the muscles in his golden throat work as he said something hoarse in his own language.

Desire roared like a furnace in his veins. The need to possess her pushed aside every other thought in his brain… It consumed him.

Her hands moved, but went back to her sides, and as he walked towards her, she regarded him steadily, her green eyes grave and almost scared.

When he was standing close enough to see the visible tremors that ran through her body he reached out and touched the side of her face.

Eva's resistance and pride melted away in the heat of the desire that roared in her blood. If he wanted her to beg she would; she could not bear the ache any longer…she was burning for his touch.

'Karim, I…'

As she tilted her face up to him Karim placed a finger on her lips before she could form her sentence.

'No,' he said, shaking his head. His treatment of Eva was not something he was proud of. Now, as he recognised he had allowed his attitude to be coloured by his experiences with Zara, he felt ashamed.

'But you said it was my—'

His hand moved to frame her face. 'I know what I said, *ma belle*,' he said thickly.

'I…'

He bent his head to her so close she could feel his warm breath on her cheek. She swayed into him as though pulled by an invisible string, her stomach muscles clenching violently in response to the warm, musky male scent of his body. 'Let me say it.'

Their glances sealed. Mesmerised by the searing heat in his

eyes, she whimpered and shivered as he stroked a finger down her cheek. Eva was so close she could see the gold tips of his eyelashes.

'Say what?'

'I will beg, Eva. I will beg for your hands on my skin…' He tilted her face to one side, his eyes running with a compulsive need over the contours of her heart-shaped face.

Holding her eyes he took her hand, wrapping his fingers in hers as he raised it to his lips. 'Touch me, Eva,' he husked, uncurling her fingers. 'Please, Princess,' he added, turning her hand over and brushing his lips across the exposed skin of her small palm.

A distracted frown creased his brow. 'You have lovely hands.'

Eva, who felt as if she were floating some place out of her body, cleared her throat. Did he really just ask what she thought he had? Or was she about to wake up?

'I like your hands too,' she responded abstractedly.

'Touch me, because if you don't I think I might lose my mind.' He looked down at her, his eyes drawn to her parted lips, and the hunger in his veins roared. He had never wanted a woman this way in his life.

Eva blinked, squeezing tears onto her cheeks as she lifted her free hand and touched his lean cheek. 'I think I lost mine some time ago,' she breathed, her expression one of fascination as she trailed a finger down his hard, stubble-roughened jaw.

He caught her hand and held it where it was and, taking the other, lifted it to his lips. 'I have dreamt, every night since we met I have dreamt of feeling your hands on me.'

The husky admission sent a fresh jolt of paralysing lust through her already shaking body. She caught her trembling lower lip between her teeth. Her passion-glazed eyes meeting his, she felt as if she were burning up from the inside out.

'I want you too, Karim.'

She watched the flare of male satisfaction blaze in his eyes before he bent his head and covered her mouth.

His heavy-lidded eyes holding her wide passion-drugged gaze, he nipped and tugged softly at her full lower lip, sliding his tongue along the soft, sensitive flesh before whispering throatily, 'You taste so sweet.' Hand on her hips, he drew her to him.

Eva gasped as his erection ground into the softness of her belly. She wound her arms around his neck as he began to kiss her, first with slow sensuality and then with a raw, driving hunger that drew a moan of pleasure from her throat.

'You're the most beautiful thing I've ever seen in my life,' he slurred.

A tiny choked sigh left her lips as she turned her head, rubbing her cheek into his palm.

'Kiss me, Karim.'

He did as if his intention were to drain her; she went limp in his arms as a debilitating weakness invaded her limbs and seeped into her brain.

Eva didn't have another coherent thought until he stopped kissing her, and then her mental coherence did not get beyond wanting him to do it again.

'Don't stop...what are you...?' Eva, finding herself excluded from the protective circle of his arms, began to protest.

The remonstration died on her lips as he proceeded to drop to his knees. Eva was briefly distracted by the sheer fluid animal grace of his action.

She could be riveted watching him do the most mundane of things.

Not that anything that was happening right now was mundane... She couldn't shake the feeling that she had slipped into some weird alternative reality and this was all happening to some other Eva.

Then as he settled in front of her, his eyes level with her bare breasts, from the place it had retreated to a strand of self-consciousness surfaced. The colour ran up like a rosy rash under her skin and she instinctively lifted her hands to cover herself.

Karim's reactions were quicker.

Before she had completed the action he grabbed her wrists and dragged them firmly back down to her sides.

Eva's hands clenched into fists as, with a groan of distress, she squeezed her eyes tight shut.

'Open your eyes and look at me, Eva.'

Obeying the command with extreme reluctance, Eva did so.

'Look at me,' he repeated.

She responded to the last instruction with even more reluctance. Karim, looking up at her with a stern expression, held her eyes and said, 'You will never cover yourself from me.'

Eva gulped. 'But—'

He shook his head. 'This is not negotiable. You are my wife and I wish to look at you and I…' His eyes swept downwards and he stopped speaking. His hands fell from her wrists as he sucked in a deep shuddering sigh.

The world around him seemed to slow as the molten heat and gnawing anger in the pit of his stomach solidified into a desire so primal that his core temperature jumped several degrees in the space of a single heartbeat.

Karim's breath came fast as he struggled to cling to the shreds of his fast disintegrating control; hunger roared in his blood like a furnace flame. They were right in front of his face: small, perfect, pouting perfection.

He dragged his eyes from the tempting curves and kissed her stomach.

Eva gasped at the touch of his tongue, then gasped again and whimpered when he traced a path with sensuous slowness up over the soft curve of her stomach, inscribing a wet line with his tongue from the hem of her pants to the valley between her heaving breasts.

The slow erotic progress drew a series of throaty moans from her aching throat. Her eyelashes fluttered against the curve of her flushed cheeks as she looked down.

'This is… Oh, my God!' she gasped, spearing her fingers into his silky dark hair. She had no conscious recollection of crying out his name, but she knew that the erotic image of his dark head against her body was burned into her brain for ever.

Hands curving around the feminine angle of her hips, he leaned back on his heels and turned his face up to her. A faint sheen of moisture covered his skin that seemed drawn tight across his incredible bones, the bands of colour along his cheekbones highlighting their prominence.

As she looked at him she was conscious of the heat pooling in her groin. 'You're…'

'What am I, Princess?'

She shook her head mutely, but her eyes communicated her feelings.

His princess, she was all woman, flesh and blood and so warm that he just wanted to lose himself in her. 'Your skin is like satin,' he husked.

The sight of her standing there above him, her perfect heaving breasts right in front of his face, took his breath away. His heart was thudding so hard he could barely hear anything above it. Part of him wanted to prolong this moment, another wanted to pull her down and slide into her welcoming heat and wetness.

Eva's head fell back and she released a broken moan as he drew her to him, fitting his mouth to one engorged nipple and drawing it into his mouth while his long fingers stroked the creamy white flesh of her quivering breast.

She bit her lip as he tugged gently at the tight bud with his teeth before lashing the glistening pink skin with his tongue, back and forth, sending white-hot stabs of sensation through her body.

A feral moan of sheer pleasure. 'That is… Oh…!'

She had reached the point where she thought she really

could no longer bear the exquisite sensual torment when he lifted his head.

He took her hands and pulled her down to him until she was on her knees facing him. One big hand slid to the small of her back, the other to the back of her bright head as he pulled her to him and slowly bent her backwards over his supporting arm.

The pressure as her sensitised breasts were crushed against his hard chest sent stabs of desire through her shaking body.

'The floor is hard,' he said, cushioning her head with his forearm. 'I'm sorry.'

'I don't care,' she panted.

Karim watched her breath coming in a series of shallow uneven gasps as with his free hand he fought his way out of his robe.

His body, curved over her in the lamplight, gleamed gold. He looked like a statue made flesh and blood. She laid her hands palms flat on his chest and closed her eyes to heighten the tactile appreciation as she allowed her fingers to glide over his skin. She reached the muscle-ridged flatness of his belly.

His gasp forced her eyes open. 'Karim, there's something I need to tell…'

Raising himself on one elbow, he curved a hand around Eva's chin and looked into her face; the flames dancing in his eyes made her dizzy.

'Later, *ma belle*. I need too—I need to kiss you. I need to taste you.'

She moaned helplessly into his mouth and writhed beneath his weight. The raw leashed power in him excited her more than she would have dreamed was possible.

His hands moving over her skin left a burning trail of desire and as his hands slid between her legs she felt no hesitation in parting them for him and pushing herself into his hand.

After a few minutes of increasingly frantic caresses he rolled a little from her and, taking her hand in his, curved it around the engorged smooth column of his erection.

'This is how much I want you, Princess. I can't wait.'

'Then don't wait,' she pleaded. 'Just please do it, Karim. I need you to do it.'

Breathing hard and holding her eyes with his, he moved over her. The moment of shock as he slid into her sucked the breath from her lungs and then as her tensed muscles relaxed and she felt him inside her, filling her, she closed her eyes.

'Oh, you are... This is so-o-o good!'

Conflicting emotions raged inside Karim, but as she tightened around him the shocked expression on his face morphed into a mask of sheer driving need.

A need to be one with her, her first. Her *only*, said the voice in his skull.

'Slow, sweetheart...slow,' he murmured, slowly moving deeper into her, then retreating again and again bringing her to the brink and thrusting deep and hard, driving her over that brink and into the dark abyss beyond.

She was vaguely conscious of Karim shuddering above her as the height of the wave of contraction hit her, drawing a shocked cry from her throat.

For a long time she floated, just letting it happen; when it stopped every cell of her body was bathed in the golden afterglow.

'Why didn't you tell me you were a virgin?'

Eva gave a grunt of complaint as he raised himself on one arm, dislodging her head from its comfortable position on his chest.

She opened her eyes and saw the accusatory note she had heard in his not quite steady voice was stamped on his dark lean features, along with a certain amount of strain that, expert that she wasn't, she didn't associate with post-coital bliss.

'I told you we didn't have sex. You didn't believe me,' she reminded him.

He dragged a not quite steady hand through his dark hair that obviously grew fast, because if he'd been wearing a collar it would have touched it.

But he wasn't, he wasn't wearing anything, and Eva was having trouble concentrating because he really was utterly perfect; every hard line of him was faultless.

'How is this possible?' He struggled to get his head around his astonishing discovery.

'I was never really into casual sex.'

'The things I said to you.'

Her lips quivered. 'It seemed to make you happy.'

'It did not,' he retorted, thinking of the images that had tortured his dreams.

'I don't think I'm a prude or anything. It's probably a low-sex-drive thing,' she mused, trailing a fascinated finger slowly down his flat muscle-ridged stomach. She felt the low rumble of laughter in his chest and lifted her head.

'What's so funny?'

Her genuine puzzlement made him laugh again, this time he followed it with a long slow kiss. 'You are.' As he appeared to like funny she could, Eva decided, live with being the butt of his private jokes.

'Is there anything else I should know?'

'Well, after that stupid row in the hospital…' She bit her lips and admitted, 'I was shocked at the idea of children, but…' her eyes fell from his '…the idea has sort of grown on me, but you seemed not to want me around.'

'I was with my father, his condition…'

Her eyes flew to his face. She saw the anguish he struggled to hide in his strong features and her heart bled for him. She lifted a hand to his cheek. 'Why didn't you tell me?'

'I am not in the habit of…sharing such things.'

'You not sharing makes me feel surplus to requirements.'

He looked visibly struck by the comment.

'Plus it made me imagine you in bed with other women.'

'There has been no room in my bed or thoughts for anyone but you lately.'

Lately—but what about the future?

Eva pushed away the intrusive thought and admitted, 'I've been thinking a little about you too.'

'You wrote a thesis!'

The indignation in his voice brought a smile to her lips. 'I polished a thesis. I even worked up the guts to come to your bedroom last night, but you weren't there.'

'You…?' The wasted opportunity drew a groan from him. 'I was out trying to sublimate my needs as I have every night since I got home.'

'With who?' she asked in a small voice.

'It depended whichever horse had not been exercised.'

'You rode.'

'Like a madman,' he admitted.

She gave a sigh of relief. 'I'm so glad, but riding at night sounds a bit reckless. You could have broken your neck.'

Karim spanned the slim column of her neck with his fingers and said, 'Aren't you glad I didn't?'

'At this moment, extremely,' she said huskily.

Karim flexed his shoulders, feeling pretty good about the world in general and what had just happened in particular. 'Why has this taken so long to happen?'

Eva curled up into his side and allowed the heat of his body to warm her cooling skin. 'Because you're stubborn and you were never there and I was embarrassed.' She tucked her head onto his chest.

Karim hooked a finger under her chin and tilted her face to his. 'Embarrassed?'

'Yes, well, how was I meant to come and beg you to take me to bed when you were obviously expecting me to be some sort of sex maniac, and I was scared stiff that I'd be a massive disappointment. To be honest, this clueless virgin thing had become a bit of an embarrassment.'

Karim, who listened to this explanation with an expression of growing fascination, laughed at the last comment.

'The fact is I didn't have sex with you that night you turned up at my flat—'

'Drugged,' Karim inserted.

'What?' she yelped.

'Long story and I prefer to hear your story now.'

'I didn't *not* have sex with you on ethical grounds. You did start to…' Her voice drifted away as the memory of the interrupted love-making rose up in her mind. 'You know.'

'I know,' he agreed, amused that she could be shy now after what they had just shared. *Sex*, reminded the voice in his head. *Don't build it up into something it isn't.* She isn't, he realized, recognising that she only spoke of sex, never love.

Which of course was a good thing.

'I'm glad we didn't, not that I was at the time,' she admitted with shamefaced honesty. 'But you'd have been m…having sex.' Just in time she caught herself before she said making love. 'But not with me…but this time it was me, wasn't it?'

'Oh, yes, it was you…*ma belle*.'

'And we are going to do it again—it won't go back to separate beds.'

'No separate beds, or separate continents, and no more stone floors, either, I think. Though possibly…' he mused. 'Once more for luck?'

'Can you? I mean…' She flushed as her eyes drifted down his body.

'I can.'

'I noticed.'

CHAPTER THIRTEEN

AMIRA'S expression as she presented Eva with the bunch of flowers brought a lump to her throat.

The little girl's dark eyes glowed with pride as she said, 'Our very first flowers.'

Eva lifted the blooms to her face to inhale the perfume that drifted off the freshly cut flowers. The little garden they had started together had begun to bloom and so had her relationship with her stepdaughter.

The problems that Eva had anticipated had never materialised. It would have been natural for the only child of a doting father, which Karim definitely was, to view her as an intruder, a rival for her father's affections, but, though she had been initially cautious and a little shy, Amira hadn't displayed any trace of jealousy.

Amira had a streak of maturity, possibly because she had spent so much time around adults, and was also amazingly perceptive for one so young.

That perception could on occasion be embarrassing—a perfect and painful example being the previous day when she had greeted her father with the remonstration, 'You're late and Eva hasn't heard a thing I've said to her for the last half-hour. She's just been looking at the door and fussing with her hair waiting for you to walk in.'

Having effectively reduced Eva to a stuttering state of hotcheeked mortification, she bounded to her feet, kissed her father and announced she would give them some privacy.

Looking at a point over Karim's left shoulder, Eva broke the ensuing silence by explaining primly, 'I overheard one of the grooms saying that the horse you were riding would break someone's neck one day and—'

'You were worried about me,' he cut in smoothly.

Eva's eyes slid to his face, her cheeks pink as she retorted indignantly, 'Who wouldn't be? I've seen you on a horse!'

And while the image of wild-eyed steed and tall rider in perfect harmony had been riveting, her pleasure had been considerably dimmed by the fact that Karim quite obviously had no concept of danger.

'I'm considered a rather good rider,' he observed with admirable understatement for someone who could have made a good living on the international polo circuit, but found the sport rather tame.

'You're reckless!' she condemned, then, lifting a hand to her hair, dealt with the child's second observation by saying, 'And I'm having a bad hair day.'

Karim walked forward and, bending his head, buried his face in her bright hair, inhaling deeply before framing her face with his hands. 'You never have a bad hair day.'

Eva had not disputed this blatantly untrue statement, partly because she had been responding to a hungry kiss that had left her aching for more.

She always ached for more.

'You were thinking about Papa.'

The comment brought Eva's wandering thoughts back to the present with a jolt.

'I…'

'You get that soppy expression and look kind of sad?'

Eva, appalled that she was so transparent even a child could see how besotted she was, pinned on a bright smile as the little girl rubbed her finger across a petal that had fallen from one of the overblown cabbage roses.

'Do they remind you of home?' asked Amira, whose curiosity about Eva's home was insatiable.

'Home?' Eva echoed, lifting a hand to a bloom and thinking back to a time when she had imagined home meant a roof and walls.

She had been brought up in reasonable affluence and had never lacked anything material, but her house had never been a home. A home, she had discovered, was being around people who made you feel good about yourself; home was about people, not bricks and mortar—people you loved.

Eva's glance encompassed the palatial surroundings that she had so recently found intimidating, surroundings that she had doubted she would ever adapt to, and she felt a little stab of shock as she recognised that this was more her *home* than anywhere she had ever lived.

'England,' the child prompted.

'They do a little,' Eva replied, wondering when she had started thinking of here as home? 'The smell more than anything.'

She did have nostalgic moments, but they never lasted long. There were too many fascinating new discoveries to make in her rich multitextured and spice-scented new world.

'And when you were young like me you grew your own garden?'

'Yes, I did,' confirmed Eva, not spoiling the story by adding that her horticultural experiment had ended abruptly when she had arrived home from school one day to find her little garden had been concreted over to provide an extra parking space.

'What garden?' had been her mother's response when she had rushed indoors in tears asking what had happened to her garden and flowers. Her mother had sat her down and explained how her emotional response was inappropriate as she had pointed out the town had ample parks but very few parking spaces. Pulling herself back to the present, she smiled at Amira.

'Now why don't you run along to your room and wash your hands while I find a really splendid vase for these lovely flowers?'

Eva followed her at a slower pace. Inside she pulled off the sunhat she wore, at Karim's insistence, to protect her fair skin from the sun, and wandered to the small sunlit sitting room that she used each morning to catch up on her correspondence—correspondence that had increased to the point where she was almost ready to agree with Karim's suggestion she take on a secretary.

Part time, maybe, she mused, would not be such an over-reaction. What had started as a casual visit to a charity that had been set up to provide education beyond school-leaving age for orphans had become something of an almost full-time commitment.

It was not something she had planned, it had just evolved, and she could not blame the organisers for roping her in when she realized, as they already had, that her name opened doors…or rather Karim's name.

And time-consuming though it had become, it was for a good cause. Eva had been forcibly struck by the shocking contrast between the opportunities that she had taken for granted at a similar age and the gratitude these young people displayed.

She had been and still was impressed by their talent, dedication and sheer determination to further their education and achieve goals that not long before would have been impossible. But with all the resolve in the world none of this would have been feasible if Karim had not continued the mission his father had begun to provide free education to every child.

And nobody wants to write about that, she thought, feeling indignant on her husband's behalf as she thought of a stupid and extremely ill-informed article printed by a magazine that was more interested in what designer he was wearing and getting his good side—as if he had a bad one—than his speech on the economic climate.

'It makes me so mad,' she muttered, putting the finishing touches to her arrangement and stepping back to view the effect.

She was tweaking a stem of greenery when her visitor was announced.

Eva had time to brush a strand of hair from her cheek and pin a smile on her face before the guest was ushered in. The smile dimmed slightly but stayed in place as her visitor was revealed to be Layla.

Six months into her marriage, Eva's feelings of insecurity had diminished considerably. She could now see Layla and Karim in the same room without wanting to scream.

She recognised that this was in small part due to the fact that when he was in her company Karim never made her feel as if he wanted to be anywhere else, and when they were apart he was also flatteringly eager to return.

But there were limits to her new confidence. She believed Karim when he said he had never had any romantic feelings for the other woman, but there was no escaping the blatantly obvious fact that Layla had feelings for him.

Eva felt the familiar prickle of antagonism and hid it behind her stiff smile as the other woman walked into the room.

The smile was not returned. Layla only put on her 'sweetness and light' act for Karim's benefit.

'I'm afraid Karim is not here.'

'I know he isn't.'

There was something feline about the smile that lifted the other woman's carmine-painted lips. Eva struggled not to feel like a defenceless mouse as Layla unsheathed her claws and added in her throaty purr, 'I came to see you.'

Eva greeted this information with deep caution. So far the other woman had shown no inclination to seek out her company—a situation that suited Eva fine.

'You did?'

Layla walked around the room, her red nails running over the polished surface of the carved chest where Eva had set her bouquet in pride of place. Her expression grew openly contemptuous as she viewed the childish offering.

'How...quaint,' she observed, looking at Eva, not the flowers.

Eva, struggling to ignore the other woman's rudeness—it wasn't normally this overt—asked quietly, 'Is there something I can help you with, Layla?'

'There's something I can help you with.'

Eva, who highly doubted this, stayed silent.

'Do you know where Karim is today?'

'He's in a meeting. They're discussing the official opening of the hospital.' As Layla's father was, she knew, to be part of this discussion group, the other woman already knew this, so why was she bringing the subject up?

Layla's expression was openly malicious as she released a tinkling laugh and said, 'Is that what he told you? Poor Eva.'

The other woman's pretended sympathy grated on Eva, who stuck out her chin and said confidently, 'Karim does not lie to me.' Sometimes she wished he would, but even in the heat of passion he never used the *L* word. 'Or discuss me with you,' she observed, quietly confident of this.

It was no big leap. It was not in her lone-wolf husband's way to share his burdens, even if his English bride was one! She had been quick to recognise the no-go areas in their relationship, but it was becoming increasingly difficult to respect the keep-off signs—difficult to stop herself making spontaneous declarations.

It had reached the point where Eva had taken to locking herself in the bathroom, turning the taps on full and allowing the water to muffle her voice as she said, 'I love you, Karim,' over and over again.

People, she had reflected on more than one occasion, had

been certified for less, but what choice did she have when she felt as if her heart would explode if she didn't say it out loud?

'But maybe he doesn't tell you the entire truth?' Layla let the suggestion hang in the air before adding, 'I think you might be the only person who doesn't know what topic is on the agenda.'

Eva, pretending boredom though her stomach was churning with sick apprehension, lifted her chin and suggested, 'Why don't you tell me what I don't know, Layla, as that seems to be the purpose of this delightful little visit?'

'Are you sure you want me to?'

Eva, who wasn't at all sure she wanted anything of the sort, snapped inelegantly, 'Spit it out, Layla.'

'They are hammering out the finer details of your separation.'

Eva looked at her with genuine incomprehension. *'Separation?'*

'Karim has no heir—'

The colour flew to Eva's cheeks. 'We've only been married six months.' She heard the defensive note in her voice and suspected from her expression that the other woman had too.

'It takes time,' Karim had said, not seeming particularly bothered when she had awkwardly brought the subject up after overhearing a conversation on the subject in the ladies' room at a function they had attended. The women had been discussing a rumour that was apparently circulating that she was already pregnant.

Karim's first response had been an eager, 'Are you?'

When she had rebutted the suggestion he had not seemed particularly put out, remarking with a bold suggestive grin that had made her pulses race that they could continue enjoying trying.

'Because you do enjoy it, don't you, *ma belle*?'

The scalding wave of helpless response as he had curled an arm around her waist and dragged her hard against him, allowing her to feel the strength of his arousal, had involved every centimetre of Eva's skin from her scalp to her toes.

Karim wanted her, his love-making left no room for doubts in that area, but he had never pretended to love her.

'And,' she added, fixing Layla with a frosty glare, 'it is a private matter.'

The older woman's pencilled brows lifted. *'Private?'* she echoed scornfully. 'You can't really be that naïve, can you?' Her vulpine lips thinned as she mused, 'Maybe not so naïve. I have to hand it to you—in landing our prince you did what many had tried and failed to do.'

Eva, who had no intention of defending her innocence to this woman, raised her brows and asked, 'Do you include yourself in that number, Layla?'

The comment earned Eva a virulent glare that made her take an involuntary step backwards; she had known the other woman disliked her, but she was only just beginning to realise how much!

'Karim would have had to marry at some point, but I saw no harm to allow him to enjoy his freedom.'

'Allow!' The woman made it sound as though she had permitted it—the woman was clearly deluded, because the only person whose feelings Karim took into account when he made a decision was his daughter…and of course his country.

Layla's eyes narrowed. 'You really think your position is so secure, don't you?' she hissed. 'Well, live in your fool's paradise while you can because your main function is to provide an heir and if you can't do that you'll be history.' She studied Eva's paper-pale face and smiled before saying confidently, 'Karim will put you aside.'

The illustrative click of her fingers made Eva start.

'And take someone who can give him an heir.'

Eva opened her mouth and closed it again. Wasn't this brutal analysis more or less the truth? Hadn't it always been, although in the last few months she had been guilty of pretending it was something else?

Had the bond she had imagined growing between them really been a figment of her wishful imagination? While she built her castles in the air she had been ignoring the fact this was and always had been a marriage of convenience.

Karim had married her because culturally and politically he'd had no choice, but if she proved to be infertile nobody, least of all her grandfather, would condemn him if he divorced her—it would be his duty.

'Someone else—you, for instance?' Eva suggested, sliding her hands into the pockets of her loose, high-waisted trousers to hide the fact they were shaking.

The other woman gave a complacent smile and ran her tongue across her glossy lips before observing. 'It is true Karim and I have always been close—*very close*,' she added, throwing a look of glittering challenge at Eva.

The overt malice shining in the other woman's eyes made Eva feel queasy. She rubbed her hands briskly across the skin of her upper arms; despite the warmth she suddenly felt chilled to the bone.

Was it possible that Layla was telling the truth? Would he discuss a subject he had avoided with her? The thought of men sitting around a table cold-bloodedly discussing, dissecting and dismantling their marriage filled Eva with utter repugnance.

'My father has brought up the topic privately. He felt it was his duty.'

Up until that point Eva, feeling pretty emotionally mauled by this conversation, had been feeling numb, but the pious addition brought a spark of anger to her green eyes.

'But actually,' the older woman drawled, 'it was Karim who suggested discussing the subject with the full council.'

Aware that the other woman was watching to see how she

reacted, Eva managed—it took every ounce of her mental reserves—to keep her face a blank canvas.

'Don't worry,' she added, her pout an indication Eva's response had not been what she'd hoped. 'I'm sure the settlement will be most generous.'

'Or I might be pregnant.' Eva slipped the comment in under the wire and watched her tormentor go pale.

'Are you?'

Eva didn't drop her gaze. 'As I have said, I feel these are matters that should stay between a husband and wife. But I do appreciate your intentions in coming here today, Layla.' Eva let the deliberately oblique comment hang in the air before she produced a brilliant smile and added, 'I will be sure to tell Karim how kind you have been.'

The vague unease in Layla's eyes became visible alarm at this prospect. 'No, really, I—'

'Now if you'll excuse me I have some things to do before Karim returns.' Her smile remained in place until she ushered the other woman from the room; the fact that Layla left looking a lot less smug than when she had arrived made the effort worthwhile.

Eva got as far as the bedroom before her composure crumbled. She closed the door and flung herself headlong on the enormous carved bed she shared with Karim.

She beat the pillows with her fists and sobbed. Finally, feeling physically and emotionally drained, she rolled on her back and stared at the carved ceiling.

Her chest lifted as she sniffed and brushed her hair back from her tear-stained face. After the emotional storm she felt drained but determined.

If she was going to leave it would be in the manner and at the time of her choosing, she decided, and the old adage no time like the present seemed rather appropriate!

At the back of one of the walk-in wardrobes—there were

five and one was bigger than her bedroom in her flat in London—she discovered the two battered suitcases she had arrived with.

She heaved them onto the bed, then, opening the nearest drawers began to pile the contents willy-nilly into them.

CHAPTER FOURTEEN

'WHAT are you doing?'

Eva spun around. The tone had been calm, almost conversational. The body language too was relaxed; Karim's broad shoulders were braced against the wall, one elegant ankle crossed casually over the other as he regarded her through half-closed eyes.

But Eva, who recognised a calm before a storm when she saw it, was not fooled. And a scene right now was just what she didn't need!

She sucked in a breath. Spine rigid, she made a deliberate show of turning her back on him before slinging him a seething glare over her shoulder.

As she returned to her task of packing Eva heard him say something that did not sound like a compliment in his native tongue.

'So I now have a personal experience of the *cold shoulder*... I cannot say I care for it.'

'And I so don't give a damn what you care about!' The frigid declaration was spoiled slightly by the quiver that crept in at the end. 'Damn!' she muttered under her breath as she dug in her pocket for a tissue and came up empty-handed.

The anger died from his face as his eyes moved from her teary eyes to her quivering lips. Despite the frustration raging in his blood, he forced himself to speak calmly as he asked, 'What are you doing?'

'You're the one with the razor-sharp intellect. I'd have thought you'd have worked it out for yourself. I'm packing.' She picked up a shoe and placed it in the overfull case, saying, 'See.' She flashed a fake smile and enunciated the word slowly. 'Pack-ing.'

'Eva…'

She ignored the warning in his deep voice, ignored the fact she could sense him moving towards her, ignored the quivering mixture of anger, self-pity and apprehension churning in her stomach and snapped without turning her head, 'I'm leaving you!'

'You are leaving me?' The information did not soothe the drumming in Karim's head.

It had been a long day and one that he had not been anticipating with any pleasure, but he was a great believer in taking the fight to the enemy and not waiting for it to knock on his door.

He had up until this point been feeling quite pleased with the results of his strategy.

'No, you are not leaving.'

Her chest swelled wrathfully as she spun around, a bra clutched in her white-knuckled hand. To find him standing so close she could feel the heat from his body made her pause, but only for a second.

'That's what you think, isn't it? You just have to say something and it will happen…or not.' She clicked her fingers, failed to produce a satisfactory click and caught his quickly repressed grin. 'Well, not this time,' she added, stabbing an accusatory finger into his broad chest.

When he remained frustratingly immune to the pressure, 'Try and stop me!' she challenged, putting all her frustration into the next jab and this time being rewarded with a satisfactory grimace for her efforts.

As she lifted an impatient hand to wipe the tears from her face Karim moved away. The expression of grim determination on his face was not reassuring.

She hung back, unsure what he was about to do. 'What... what are you...?'

Maintaining his silence, Karim held her eyes while he slammed the lid of one suitcase closed. 'Leave that alone.'

He flashed her a grim smile and slammed the second shut.

The power struggle was over before it began, but Eva made a determined effort to cling to the case that Karim already had in his possession. Karim barely seemed to notice her efforts as he casually tugged it out of her grasp and hefted the other beneath his free arm.

As she staggered backwards Eva watched him stride to the open window and onto the wrought-iron balcony.

'What are you doing, Karim? Stop... Oh, my God!' She gasped, staring in disbelief as he quite deliberately emptied the contents of one case over the balcony into the courtyard below. He then threw the case after it.

'The method is crude,' he admitted, flashing her a dangerous grin as he began to dish out identical treatment to the second case. 'But you did invite me to stop you.'

'You're mad!' she yelled, rushing out to the balcony in time to see the second case land in a fountain. Her belongings, for the most part underclothes and shoes—not all pairs; her packing had not been exactly methodical—were scattered around the courtyard.

'Why were you leaving?'

Eva carried on staring at a pair of her knickers—red silk ones that had brought a gleam to Karim's eyes when he saw her wearing them. No more red knickers—they were torn, hanging from the branch of an orange tree. And no more gleams, she thought dully.

'Eva...?'

Eva straightened her shoulders and took a deep breath before she turned to face him. '*Am* leaving, *am*—wrong tense.'

'Don't be ridiculous, Eva.'

Her temper fizzed. 'At least I'll never be patronised by you again.' Or kissed, or taken to the stars and back, or told in a voice that melted her bones that she was beautiful… 'And as for those…' she nodded to her belongings '…I'll go in what I stand up in. I really don't care.' *And where will you go, Eva?* asked the voice in her head.

'Why, Eva?'

She gulped and blinked away a fresh rush of tears, turning her head from the tenderness in his eyes. It was all a lie and she was a fool because she had believed it. 'It's better to jump than be pushed.'

His brow furrowed in irritation. 'Pushed? What do you mean "pushed"?'

'There's no need to pretend, Karim.'

The only thing Karim was pretending was that he was in control, and that pretence was wearing pretty thin.

'I know about your meeting.'

Karim, in the act of reaching out to pull her to him, froze.

'How many months did you decide on before I'm officially designated barren?'

He flinched, but said nothing.

Eva, ignoring the danger signals of the nerve jumping in his lean cheek and the white line etched around his sensual lips, interpreting his lack of reaction as guilt, added, 'I'm curious—what is the market value of a discarded infertile wife? One that has all her own teeth, that is I'm given to understand that the settlement can be quite generous?'

Eva had thought she had seen him angry before, but the flash of sheer molten fury that blazed from his eyes as they connected with her own was on a different scale. Every muscle and sinew in his body was drawn tight as, with a face like a carved bronze statue, he took a step towards her.

'*Mon Dieu*, you will not speak of yourself that way—is that understood?'

Eva took a wary step backwards, which took her perilously close to the edge of the balcony. She cast a sideways glance towards the drop and felt dizzy. She turned her face to an ablaze Karim and felt dizzier.

He was awesome, six feet five of smouldering virile masculinity. As they stared at one another he tore the headdress from his head and flung it to one side before raking a frustrated hand through his glossy hair.

'Do you ever stop and think before you act?'

'That's rich coming from you. You could have killed someone,' she condemned piously as she nodded towards the courtyard. He was killing her just by standing this close. The scent of his skin, as well as driving her quietly nuts, was eating steadily into her resolve to leave.

'They could have ducked,' Karim retorted, displaying a callous lack of concern for any victims of his outburst. 'And the last time I checked a bra is not a deadly weapon.'

Unless Eva was wearing it, he corrected, his eyes drifting to her heaving bosom that appeared interestingly unfettered beneath the drifty silk blouse thing she was wearing. The soft green brought out the darker emerald of her eyes; it also did little to disguise the small pointed perfection of her breasts.

Momentarily distracted—for a man who was renowned for his powers of concentration that was happening a lot—by the image that formed in his head of his brown fingers, dark in contrast to the warm creamy mound of silken flesh they caressed, his glance lingered as lust licked like a flame along his receptive nerve endings.

Sticking out her chin, Eva succeeded to some degree in hiding her apprehension, but her composure crumbled when she saw where his heavy-lidded stare rested. Her bolshy attitude tipped over into dismay as she recognised the familiar illicit jolt of excitement that crept through her body.

Karim's jaw was set as he wrenched his gaze upwards. 'Who…who said this to you?' he demanded thickly. 'Who mentioned *divorce*?'

She shook her head mutely.

His lips compressed, a muscle beside his clenched jaw jumped. 'I will know.'

Eva shook her head; in an unrealistic corner of her heart she had hoped he would deny it. It was irrational to feel so utterly betrayed, but she couldn't help it.

A harder shell was what she needed she told herself. Being an old-fashioned romantic who loved a happy ending left you open to all sorts of pain in the real no-happy-ever-after-ending world.

'It doesn't matter who told me,' she said dully. He wasn't mad because it was a lie, he was mad because she had found out—presumably before he was ready.

His eyes narrowed. 'I think I know who it was.' Layla would wait, he decided, turning his attention to his wife. He bent his head towards her, brushing aside a hank of dark hair that fell into his eyes as he laid a hand on her shoulder and rubbed his thumb over the elegant angle of her delicate collarbone, and felt a shiver run through her body.

Karim felt a sharp, sweet, heart-piercing stab of tenderness. She looked so incredibly fragile, but he knew that the fragility concealed a strong, fiery woman with passions to match his own.

A woman who was so responsive to his touch that the brush of his breath on her neck could elicit a wild reaction—his cousin had recently called him a lucky man; he was not wrong.

As she tilted her head and their eyes connected her body swayed towards him as though drawn by an invisible thread. His eyes darkened as for a heartbeat he was totally submerged by a wave of mingled tenderness, lust and wonderment.

'Sit down and let me explain, *ma belle*.'

His mesmerising voice flowed over her like honey.

'Let me explain…?'

And I'll believe him because I want to… With a self-derisive grimace Eva shook her head to clear the sensual fog that clouded her brain.

'You mean lie down!' she snarled. 'Because you think all you have to do is get me in bed and I'll swallow any garbage you dish up.' And so far she had, she had let him make her feel as though she were beautiful and desirable. 'I'm not beautiful and I don't need anything explained. I understand perfectly.'

'I doubt that.'

The odd inflection in his voice brought her frowning regard to his face.

'Beautiful…?' Head tilted a little to one side, he studied her face. Several strands of hair had fallen across her smooth brow, the rest was tied back in a utilitarian plait he had noticed she confined it in when she intended to be taken seriously.

The silence stretched until, unable to bear his critical appraisal another second, she snapped, 'My mouth is too big, my nose is too small, my eyes are—'

'Incredible.' The eyes in question widened to their fullest extent at the throaty insertion.

Eva pressed a hand to her fluttering heart; she was such a pushover.

'Beauty,' he continued, 'is a word. I just know that I like waking up looking at your face.' Like was too mild a word for the life-affirming jolt he got when he woke up and found her beside him.

A little thrown off balance, not just by his comment, but his intense tone, she gave a disgruntled sniff and drawled, 'Sure, I'm utterly perfect.'

Karim gave a twisted smile and, planting both hands firmly on her shoulders, steered her firmly away from the wrought-iron rail.

Eva kept up a flat-toned narrative while he steered her to a chair—it was either that or an unseemly tussle. It was hard to occupy the moral high ground when you were kicking a person's shins.

'*Perfect* but not the wife you would have chosen, but you needed one at some point anyway because you need an heir.'

'Is that a direct quote from Layla?' Karim wondered, thinking that he had been a fool to allow that woman the run of the place just because of who her father was.

Eva looked startled and gave a little grunt as, in response to the weight of his hands on her shoulders, she sat down heavily on the chair.

'If I don't give you a baby,' she pressed a hand to her stomach and struggled to control the wobble in her voice as she finished gruffly, 'nobody, not even my grandfather, would blame you if you put me aside for someone who could. I knew all this…'

I just chose not to think too much about it, she thought, ashamed of her inability to face the truth. 'But what I didn't know, what makes me feel…' She shuddered and buried her face in her hands. Exhaling and lifting her pale face to his, she backtracked, forming the words slowly as if each syllable hurt as she continued, 'What I didn't know is that I would be a topic on an agenda and you would discuss me like any other piece of business with those men….'

'So you thought you would anticipate matters and run away? Were you going to leave a note?'

Eva winced at the bitter irony in his voice.

'You are right—I would not have chosen you.' It was hard now to credit that he had ever been that stupid.

He saw her flinch and dropped down into a squatting position by her chair. 'But I *have* you.' And he intended to keep her. He would not, *could* not contemplate life without her.

The emotional throb in his deep voice brought Eva's head up.

She looked at him warily as he framed her face in his big hands and blotted a tear that slid down her cheek with his thumb. 'I do not question this and lie awake wondering about the chain of events that made this happen, I do not speculate on whether cosmic fate, luck, or sheer chance played a part. I accept it and never *ever* stop being grateful for it.' The impassioned declaration made Eva's heart stop.

Did eyes, the window of the soul, lie? Karim's were saying things that she hardly dared believe, things that contradicted everything.

'Grateful?' Then she shook her head and told herself she was just seeing what she wanted to. 'You made arrangements, drew up contracts, to get rid of me... How long have I got? Six months...a year...?' She shook her head and tried to pull his hands from her face; somehow her fingers got tangled in his and ended up pressed to his heart.

She could feel the thud through the thin cotton robe he wore over riding breeches. The need to press herself into the warmth of his body was so overwhelming that not doing so made her shake like someone with a fever.

'I am expected to provide an heir. This is not an unreasonable expectation,' he conceded. 'You want children...?'

Her eyes fell from his. 'Yes!' she admitted, her voice thick with the emotion that clogged her throat.

'Then where is the problem?'

She tipped her head to him, incredulous that he seemed unable to understand why she was upset.

He dragged a hand across the morning growth of stubble on his chin and shook his dark head. 'I found you packing your bags and looking at me as though I was your enemy. I'm not, Eva, you're my lover, my wife...'

'Not a popular choice.'

He arched a brow and did not deny it. 'This meeting was not what you think. Forget what Layla told you and listen to me!'

The antagonistic glitter faded from Eva's eyes. She slanted him a guarded look through her lashes and nodded. 'All right, tell me.'

He watched with a half-smile as she folded her arms across her chest and adopted an unimpressed expression.

'You look like a tough audience,' he observed.

Eva fought back an answering smile. 'I'm an objective audience,' she lied.

'There are some, fewer than you might think, in high positions who consider you an unsuitable bride.' Those in short who had personal interests to preserve and blamed his new wife's influence for some recently introduced reforms that had impacted on their pockets—those changes had been planned for some time.

Political manoeuvring was a fact of life, but when Karim had learnt of the whispering campaigns targeting Eva that had been set in motion his first response had been to make the worthless, avaricious scum eat their lies and hopefully choke on them.

But when he had been able to consider the situation in a slightly cooler frame of mind—it had taken a half-day gallop across the desert on a hot-blooded stallion that had been badly in need of exercise to achieve this—he had realised that they had unwittingly done him a favour.

They had forced him to take the initiative.

And he had done so with relish.

It hadn't actually been so difficult; his opponents had always been on shaky ground. It spoke volumes of how well his inexperienced princess bride was fulfilling her role that their grievances were so easy to demolish.

Of course, the suggestion that Eva not being pregnant after a few months was a problem—or, for that matter, any of their business—was total nonsense, and he had summarily disposed of it as such.

'I knew they were planning to present me with an ultimatum.' His lips curved into a smile that contained a degree of wolfish relish as he recalled their faces when he had turned the tables. 'I beat them to it.'

Eva felt her body turn to ice and stared at him, unable to

credit the casual callousness. 'So you told them you'd already decided to divorce me.' Amazing—there was nothing in her composed voice to suggest someone had just broken her heart and stamped all over it.

Above her bowed head she heard his sharp intake of breath and angry curse. 'If you carry on speaking of divorce, *ma belle*, I will begin to think that is what you wish…' With a finger under her chin, he angled Eva's face up to his. 'I told them there would be no divorce.'

The smile that began to curve Eva's lips faded abruptly when she saw how it must have been.

Those men were not bright. She had only known Karim for a few months, but it had taken her about five minutes to work out her proud husband was not a man you gave ultimatums.

He was a man who would dig his feet in and if possible go in the opposite direction, even if that direction was not in his best interests.

'But why did you say that?' she wailed.

This had been the point where, in his mind at least, she had thrown herself in his arms… He inhaled and stifled his frustration. 'This was not the response I was hoping for, *ma belle*.' Though he spoke lightly there was a steely glint in his eyes as he added, 'You still wish to pack your bags and escape me?'

She gave a twisted smile that just about broke his heart and said huskily, 'Well, that would simplify matters all around.'

'There has been nothing simple about our relationship from day one.' He ran a finger down her damp cheek. 'You said you wanted a child, our child…children?'

There had been no *of course* before she fell in love with Karim, but now she responded without thinking. 'Of course I do, but what if I can't have them? You'll have no choice but to divorce me, Karim.'

'There is always a choice.'

'Look, I know it's the worst-case scenario, but—'

He pressed a finger to her lips and said, 'Fine worst-case

scenario—if I could not give you the child you crave would you send me away?'

Her eyes widened indignantly. 'Of course not!'

'Do you not see the inconsistency here?'

Eva flung him a look of teary reproach. 'It's different.'

'Where is the difference?' He took her chin in his hand and tipped her face up to his. 'Look at me, Eva, and tell me where the difference is in these two scenarios. Never losing sight of the fact we are discussing something that will never happen.'

'You can't know that—' she began.

Only to be cut off by his terse direction to, 'Tell me, why do you have one set of rules for yourself and another for me, Princess?'

The warmth in his eyes made Eva's heart tremble in her breast. As he reached out to stroke her cheek she knew she should pull away, but she couldn't. She turned her face into his palm and closed her eyes.

'The thought of people talking about me makes me feel so…' She gave a shudder.

His eyes darkened and his voice was soothing as he replied, 'I know.'

'What would you know about how it feels? Everyone knows you can have a child—you already do. You have Amira.'

'Ah!' He exhaled a deep breath and pressed her face into his chest as he rested his chin on her sweet-smelling hair and inhaled.

Eva sighed as his arms closed around her. She wanted to stay there for ever but she knew this couldn't happen. She experienced a swell of sadness that took her breath away, then abruptly the sadness morphed into anger. She was so mad she couldn't breathe as she pulled away from him and, knocking the chair over, shot to her feet.

She was angry with Karim for making him love her, but most of all she was mad with herself for falling in love and for pretending that this marriage was anything but a convenient contract.

Stormy eyes shining with suppressed emotion that threatened like the tears standing out in them to spill over, she stood there vibrating so much emotion that Karim, standing feet away, felt it hit him like a wave.

'I have Amira,' he agreed. '*We* have Amira.'

Eva's face crumpled. If she had to go away she would miss the little girl she had grown to love.

'It would have been better if we'd never met!'

Eva bit her lip, retaining an air of defiance, but feeling regret when the skin stretched tight across the strong symmetrical bones of his face paled dramatically.

Despite the visible effect of her bitter claim, his expression appeared to be utterly confident as he shook his head and said, 'No, it wouldn't. You love me, Eva.'

If it had been a taunt she would have been able to cling to her anger, but it wasn't. It was just a quiet statement of fact, and instead it sliced through her defences.

Her lip quivered. 'Yes, I love you, Karim… I didn't mean to…' Her expression one of stunned bewilderment, she shook her head and admitted, 'I tried not to.'

CHAPTER FIFTEEN

KARIM let his head fall back as he expelled a long shuddering sigh and murmured something in his own tongue.

Appalled that she had allowed him to goad her into the admission, Eva adopted a shaky air of belligerence as she waited for his response. So far it wasn't easy to predict.

He lifted his head. There was an air of satisfaction bordering on smugness in his manner as he smiled; the indefinable but dangerous quality to that smile made Eva's stomach flutter nervously.

'If it is any comfort I also tried not to... I didn't want to love you, I tried not to love you, but I stopped trying.'

For a long moment they just stared at one another, then with a sob she walked into the arms he held open. His lips on hers, Karim lifted her off her feet and twirled her around.

His exuberant cry of triumph sent an answering wild, joyful thrill through Eva. She wrapped her legs around his waist and, holding his face between her hands, kissed him back with enthusiasm.

His deep husky laugh rang out as he kissed her back. Still kissing, they fell onto the bed together. The kissing continued, punctuated by gasps, murmurs and moans, until they both paused to catch their breath.

Lying side by side, heart to heart, Eva smiled; the exhilaration singing through her blood was more intoxicating than champagne.

'You love me, I'm irresistible, so are you,' she crooned, her eyes darkening as she slid her hand across the exposed golden skin of his throat, her fingertips lingering on his pulse. She slid him a smoky look from under the sweep of her lashes and said with mock innocence, 'Don't you feel a little overdressed?'

'No, Eva,' he said, catching her hand and pressing it to his lips to lessen the impact of his rejection. 'First I must tell you something that I should have told you before now.'

The sombreness of his expression brought an apprehensive frown to Eva's face. 'So tell me,' she suggested, propping herself up on her elbow. She could deal with anything he threw at her so long as he loved her.

And he did.

Karim loved her.

'It is something that nobody knows with the exception,' he said quietly, 'of possibly Hakim.' Hakim was no fool and he had asked some pretty searching medical questions after the failure to find a bone-marrow donor for Amira. 'It is important that the secret stays with us, *mon coeur*.'

'Of course,' Eva said, beginning to feel both impatient and seriously worried after this build-up. She reached across and stroked the side of his lean face. 'Tell me,' she urged, thinking, *Please let me have my happy ending, please*. 'It doesn't matter what it is, I'll still love you, but tell me soon because I have to tell you, Karim, you're scaring me,' she admitted.

'Amira is not my child.'

Eva's face went blank. Of all the things she had been bracing herself to hear, this had not been one of them.

Thoughts racing, she rolled closer, looping her thigh over his hip and tucking herself into his side as she asked with genuine mystification, 'How is that possible?'

'You know that my first marriage was arranged.'

She nodded. 'She was very beautiful.'

He did not appear to notice the wistful comment. 'Zara told me on our wedding night.'

Still not understanding, Eva shook her head. 'She told you what?'

'That she was carrying another man's child.'

'Oh, no, Karim! On your…you must have been devastated!' Eva gasped, still struggling to get her head around the information.

It required a seismic mental shift. The perfect marriage she had always imagined she was competing with, the one that made her feel woefully inadequate, had been based on a lie, and what a lie!

She felt her astonishment give way to anger—how could any woman do that to a man, callously trap him that way? Force him to bring up another man's child as his own?

She supposed that there must be many men out there bringing up children who were not genetically theirs, but the difference was that Karim had known it—always known it.

Her eyes glowed with admiration as she looked at Karim through an emotional mist of tears. Some men might have punished the child for the sins of the mother, rejected them, but never by one word or action had he ever treated Amira as anything but his own. How many men were that generous, that bighearted?

'Devastated, no…' he conceded after a moment's silent consideration of the suggestion. 'Humiliated and furious—yes. My pride was hurt. No man likes to feel a woman has made a fool of him. Since then I have been inclined to think guilty until proved innocent…as you, *ma belle,* learnt to your cost,' he observed with a rueful grimace of self-reproach.

'That night when I realised you were an innocent,' he recalled huskily, 'I think was the first time I realised what I had become, what I had let one bad experience make me,' he admitted soberly. 'A man who only sees the bad and not the good…' His loving gaze swept her face. 'You have re-educated me.'

'It was quite a *big* bad experience, Karim, and,' she added, nipping gently at the curve of his beautiful mouth, 'you have educated me too.' She let her bold sultry gaze linger on his mouth and added with a throaty chuckle, 'And I rather enjoyed the instruction. You're a *very* good teacher.'

Not proof against this form of provocation, with a groan Karim slid her beneath him, pinning her arms either side of her face, and fitted his mouth to hers.

It was several breathless minutes later that Karim resumed his story.

'I was trapped into a loveless marriage and after seven years of celibacy—' He nuzzled his nose against hers before pulling back a little to drink in her face, taking in each feature and the smooth curve of her cheek. 'You are adorable,' he breathed, lifting a strand of hair from her cheek to give him access to her smooth throat. Eva's eyelids dropped and her breath came in fluttering sighs as he kissed his way towards her mouth. Once there he looked into her half-closed eyes with such glowing adoration shining in his that her heart stood still as he pressed a butterfly kiss to each corner of the soft, quivering curve.

'There was nobody else?' Her expression was dreamy as she forced the words past the aching lump in her throat. 'I really can't believe this is happening…' She stopped abruptly in the act of pulling his head down and her eyes flew wide. '*Seven years*! You didn't have sex for seven years.'

'This surprises you? That I would respect the vows I made…?'

'Oh, no, it isn't that,' she rushed to assure him. She had learnt pretty early that, far from being the shallow playboy stereotype the media liked to paint him, Karim possessed strong moral principles. Sometimes she thought he took it too far. 'It's just that's a long time and you're very…' She stopped, feeling the heat climb to her cheeks.

Would there ever be a day, she wondered in frustration, when she *didn't* blush like a schoolgirl?

Karim arched a brow and grinned broadly at her discomfiture. 'I am?' he prompted.

Feeling the laughter vibrating in his chest, she batted his ear playfully and said, 'All right, you're such an animal in bed I can't imagine you going two days without sex, let alone seven years!' Eva teased, only half joking.

'Thank you,' he said, no longer hiding his amusement. 'But it is you, my little one, who brings out the beast in me. Actually a man can channel his energies.' He stopped, the sardonic smile fading from his face as he looked at her.

'The truth is there has never been anything in my life I could not control, including my emotions and libido—until I met you. I have wondered recently if I would have been able to show such nobility and self-sacrifice if I had met you while I was still married. To find you and be unable to claim you as my own would have been, I think...more than I could bear.'

Moved to the point of tears by his admission, she curved her hands around his face. 'Well, it didn't happen that way around. You'd already been on the open market for some time and from what I have heard you made up for lost time.'

He accepted the caustic observation with a wolfish grin. 'I must admit then I was enjoying my freedom. I knew that marriage was necessary but I was in no hurry and then...'

'Then I trapped you in my web.'

'Do not remind me what I said!' he begged. 'I was a fool!' he observed, rolling onto his back and pulling her on top of him.

Eva planted her hands either side of his face, and gazed down into his dark features, a bemused frown creasing her smooth brow. 'Why did she do it, Karim? Why did she marry you if she already had a lover?'

'It was a simple matter of expedience. She said there was no chance of this man she loved marrying her and marriage to me was the only way to avoid disgrace. She was,' he recalled drily, 'very frank. She said she had considered not telling me and letting me think the baby was mine, but she decided to tell me the truth.'

'A bit late in the day to have a crisis of conscience!' Eva exclaimed, utterly appalled on his behalf.

He conceded this with a shrug, feeling the throb of desire as he spread his fingers over the curve of one perfect breast. Above him Eva closed her eyes and gave a small gasp of pleasure.

'It was not conscience that made her reveal her condition, but a repugnance at the idea of sharing my bed.'

If Eva had ever had any doubts she now knew the woman had been barking mad!

'She did offer to fulfil her wifely duties after the baby was born,' he admitted, grimacing at the memory. 'But I passed.'

'You didn't sleep with her ever?'

He shook his head.

Eva rolled away from him and, arm curved above her head, stared at the ceiling as she reeled slightly under the impact of the revelations. It was particularly ironic when you considered how she had been tormented by the conviction that every time she screwed up Karim was comparing her with his perfect first wife.

'Who is Amira's father?'

'I am, Eva.'

Eva turned her head and smiled lovingly. 'I know…did anyone ever suspect?'

'Obviously the hospital knew—that was inevitable. The blood tests proved that I could not be her biological father… completely ruling me out as a possible bone-marrow donor.' The inability had at the time driven him to despair.

'And Hakim.'

'He was the one who initially diagnosed Amira. I think he suspects, but I know he would say nothing. Zara never told me who the father was and I did not ask. All I know is that he was a married man.'

'What did you do…say…when she told you?' It was a scenario that Eva could not even imagine.

'What could I say? Our marriage was a sham. The only good thing to come out of it was Amira. I was determined to do my duty, but I never expected to feel genuine attachment, paternal feelings for another man's child,' he admitted. 'But when she was born and I held her the bonding—it was instant. Zara went through the motions but she wanted a boy…she never really forgave Amira for being a girl.'

Eva's horror at the lack of maternal feeling showed in her expression as she shook her head and said, 'How could any mother…? I just don't understand….'

'Of course you don't,' he said, his deep voice thick with emotion as he wrapped his arms tight around her. 'You will love our babies unconditionally. You will forgive them anything just as you have forgiven me.'

'Did she ever see him again, her lover?'

Karim gave an uninterested shrug. 'Possibly. She took lovers during our marriage but she was always discreet.'

Eva did not hide her astonishment. 'And you didn't care?'

He nodded. 'Why would I? But do not let this give you any ideas, *mon coeur*. I would not be similarly disinterested if you ever looked at another man.'

Eva laughed at the absurdity of the idea and teased, 'Then you'll just have to make sure I don't get bored with you.'

'I bore you?'

'You…' She paused, the teasing light fading from her eyes as her voice dropped a husky emotional octave. 'You complete me, Karim. You make me a whole person. I think without you I would fade away and not exist at all.'

His eyes darkened with passion as he murmured her name. 'Before I met you I believed…I believed in duty in a man's ability to shape his future, but I didn't believe in anything I could not touch and feel. I did not believe in love, then you came into my life and all that changed.

'At this meeting today I told them that should we not be able to conceive at a time of my choosing I would step down... abdicate.'

Eva stared at him, convinced she had misheard. 'Why would you do that...?' She shook her head, her thoughts in a whirl. What he was saying made no sense. Karim's duty to his country and his people would always be an integral part of him.

'I don't believe it.'

Karim's lips curled into a grim smile. His advisors had not, either, and when they had realised that he meant what he said they had suddenly become less eager to set a deadline.

'You couldn't abdicate. This is your life.'

'You are my life. I would give my life for my land, the people, but without you beside me I have not the...' He swallowed as he lifted his shining eyes to her face. He struggled to control his erratic breathing as he placed a hand to his heaving chest and husked. 'Heart!' His voice dropped to a whisper. 'I would not have the heart to do this alone, Eva. You are my heart and my strength.

'If they want me, I come as a package and if I fail to supply an heir I will be honour-bound to step down and it will be Hakim's turn. Our playboy doctor must take the helm.'

'I can't let you do this, Karim,' she gasped.

'I am doing nothing but give myself permission to love you. Would you deny me this, *mon coeur*? My life has been all about duty up to this point—have I not a right to be selfish?'

'You say this now and I know you believe it, but if...' she sniffed, struggling to hold back the tears '...if we don't have a baby and you do this, you throw it all away, you will grow in time to resent me. This country to you is like...like...it's like the Church is to a priest.'

He looked startled. 'A bad-fitting analogy,' he chided with a laugh. 'I am not priest material. And do not believe that I don't understand your fears,' he added gently. 'But,' he told her firmly, 'this is not about sacrifice. I have my family—you and Amira. My country will survive without me but I will not survive without you. The equation is that simple. Life is at its heart that simple.'

Eva listened to his impassioned words with tears of emotion flowing unchecked down her cheeks. She could not believe this incredible man loved her that much. 'And I can't survive without you, Karim,' she whispered.

'Then do not cry. I cannot bear to see you cry, Eva. There is nothing to cry about. I see you with a baby in your arms.'

Eva gave a wistful sigh. 'I hope so.'

'Hope does not make babies,' he said, drawing her to him. 'But I know what does.'

'You do?'

'I do, *ma belle*,' he confirmed, smiling deep into her eyes.

She kissed the corner of his beautiful mouth and rubbed her nose against his. 'Show me?'

'I thought you'd never ask!' he sighed with a grin.

Nine months later Karim was regretting his success in the baby department.

He had read all the books. He had attended all the classes. He had felt confident and well equipped to cope with what was to come; he had been looking forward to it...!

And then Eva had gone into labour and nothing had followed the plan he had helped her write and nobody seemed particularly surprised.

It also quickly became obvious that all the literature skimmed too lightly over the pain part; nothing had prepared him for watching his wife endure agony for hours on end. Amira had been born by a forceps delivery and he had not been allowed in the room.

And the female doctors and midwives appeared to respond to everything he said with the same patronising smile.

And the helplessness, that was the worst—to watch her suffer and not be able to do anything about it.

He closed his eyes as, when urged to push by the doctor, Eva let out a cry that made his blood freeze.

And nobody seemed to act as if this were anything untoward!

It was clearly time he took charge.

'I think she needs a Caesarean. There are obviously complications.'

The doctor smiled; they were all so damned cheerful. 'Your wife is doing extremely well, Prince Karim.'

'Karim,' Eva gasped. 'Will you please sit down? I'm trying to concentrate.'

'But…?'

'Just do it, Karim.'

Recognising the tone, he did as she requested. He had barely taken his place beside the bed when the doctor said, 'The head is crowning…the next contraction…push hard.'

In the final stages his fascination overcame his fear, and as Karim watched his son being born his eyes filled with tears. It was the most emotional moment of his life, until ten minutes later when his daughter followed her brother into the world screaming loudly and sporting a full head of bright red hair.

'Oh, you poor little love,' Eva said when her daughter was placed in her arms. 'You got the hair.' Her son had been born as dark as his father.

Carrying his firstborn, Karim sat down on the bed beside her and looked into the perfect face of his daughter. 'She's beautiful,' he said, raising his voice to be heard above her shrill cries.

'And loud,' Eva added with a smile as she lifted the blanket to take another look at their son.

'You were marvellous, Eva, incredible,' he said, pressing a long lingering kiss to her lips. 'That,' he added, expelling a long shuddering sigh, 'was the best and worst thing that has ever happened to me.'

Eva looked up at her handsome husband, the love shining like a beacon in her eyes.

'You're the best thing that has ever happened to me, Karim. Nine months to the day,' she added with a naughty smile. 'When you decide to make a baby you really don't do half measures, do you?'

'I must admit I did not foresee this level of success.'

Eva, weary but glowing with contentment, leaned back into the pillows. 'I remember the look on your face when they said it was twins.' The sheer panic on her normally über-controlled husband's face had been priceless.

'It was hot in that room, very poorly ventilated.' He broke off and grinned. 'I thought I was ready for this…I was so wrong. I'm sorry….'

'You were fantastic, the perfect distraction from the pain,' she added with a teasing smile. 'Though the staff might not agree,' she admitted.

'Shall I fetch Amira?'

'Please. How about you give that one to me and you go and fetch their big sister?'

Karim placed the baby carefully in the crook of her free arm and, looking back at the picture they made, paused and sighed. 'I really am the luckiest man in the world. Remind me to give Tariq a raise for drugging me.'

'Tariq would work for you for free,' she told him with a laugh. 'And you know it.'

A few minutes later, with her husband by her side, her babies in her arms and their sister holding their hands with an expression of awed wonder on her face, Eva found herself echoing Karim's sentiments.

'*We're* the luckiest people in the world,' she said huskily.

Karim bent over and kissed her until he was obliged to stop to allow Eva to attend to her noisy daughter.

'You don't suppose she's going to do that every time I kiss

you, do you?' Karim asked as he watched Eva put the baby to her breast.

'Are you all right?' Eva asked, her eyes on his face.

'The sheer miracle of it all kept coming over me in waves,' he admitted. 'I still can't believe we came in as three this morning and we'll go home tomorrow as five.'

'You promised me a miracle, Karim, and you delivered.' And he would, she knew, carry on doing just that. Eva gave a contented sigh. She knew she could face whatever the future might hold with her husband at her side.

He looked at her tired face and felt his heart swell. 'Now I am going to deliver on some sleep. Give me those two,' he said, consulting his watch. 'And do not think of moving for the next two hours.'

'Is that a royal command?'

'It's a humble request.'

Eva gave a sleepy laugh. Her husband did not do humble, but he did everything else extremely well indeed, she thought, closing her eyes.

★

⊚™ MILLS & BOON®

are proud to present our...

Book of the Month

★

Snowbound:
Miracle Marriage
★
by Sarah Morgan from
Mills & Boon® Medical™

Confirmed bachelor Dr Daniel Buchannan is
babysitting his brother's children and needs help!
Stella, his ex-fiancée, reluctantly rescues him and,
snowbound with his makeshift family, Daniel
realises he can never let Stella go again…

Enjoy double the romance in this
great-value 2-in-1!
Snowbound: Miracle Marriage
&
Christmas Eve: Doorstep Delivery
by Sarah Morgan

Mills & Boon® Medical™
Available 4th December 2009

Something to say about our
Book of the Month?
Tell us what you think!
millsandboon.co.uk/community

millsandboon.co.uk Community

Join Us!

The Community is the perfect place to meet and chat to kindred spirits who love books and reading as much as you do, but it's also the place to:

- Get the inside scoop from authors about their latest books
- Learn how to write a romance book with advice from our editors
- Help us to continue publishing the best in women's fiction
- Share your thoughts on the books we publish
- Befriend other users

Forums: Interact with each other as well as authors, editors and a whole host of other users worldwide.

Blogs: Every registered community member has their own blog to tell the world what they're up to and what's on their mind.

Book Challenge: We're aiming to read 5,000 books and have joined forces with The Reading Agency in our inaugural Book Challenge.

Profile Page: Showcase yourself and keep a record of your recent community activity.

Social Networking: We've added buttons at the end of every post to share via digg, Facebook, Google, Yahoo, technorati and de.licio.us.

www.millsandboon.co.uk

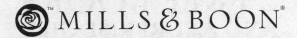

2 FREE BOOKS
AND A SURPRISE GIFT

We would like to take this opportunity to thank you for reading this
Mills & Boon® book by offering you the chance to take TWO more
specially selected books from the Modern™ series absolutely FREE!
We're also making this offer to introduce you to the benefits of the
Mills & Boon® Book Club™—

- **FREE home delivery**
- **FREE gifts and competitions**
- **FREE monthly Newsletter**
- **Exclusive Mills & Boon Book Club offers**
- **Books available before they're in the shops**

Accepting these FREE books and gift places you under no obligation to buy, you may cancel at any time, even after receiving your free
books. Simply complete your details below and return the entire page
to the address below. You don't even need a stamp!

YES Please send me 2 free Modern books and a surprise gift. I
understand that unless you hear from me, I will receive 4 superb new
books every month for just £3.19 each, postage and packing free. I
am under no obligation to purchase any books and may cancel my
subscription at any time. The free books and gift will be mine to keep
in any case.

Ms/Mrs/Miss/Mr_____ Initials _____

Surname _____
Address _____

_____ Postcode _____

Send this whole page to: Mills & Boon Book Club, Free Book Offer,
FREEPOST NAT 10298, Richmond, TW9 1BR

Offer valid in UK only and is not available to current Mills & Boon Book Club subscribers to this series.
Overseas and Eire please write for details. We reserve the right to refuse an application and
applicants must be aged 18 years or over. Only one application per household. Terms and prices subject to
change without notice. Offer expires 28th February 2010. As a result of this application, you may receive
offers from Harlequin Mills & Boon and other carefully selected companies. If you would prefer not to
share in this opportunity please write to The Data Manager, PO Box 676, Richmond, TW9 1WU.

Mills & Boon® is a registered trademark owned by Harlequin Mills & Boon Limited.
Modern™ is being used as a trademark. The Mills & Boon® Book Club™ is being used as a trademark.